DIAMONDS IN THE ROUGH

DIAMONDS ARE FOREVER TRILOGY (BOOK 2)

CHARMAINE PAULS

Published by Charmaine Pauls

Montpellier, 34090, France

www.charmainepauls.com

Published in France

This is a work of fiction. Names, characters, and incidents depicted in this book are products of the author's imagination or are used fictitiously. Any resemblance to actual events, locales, organizations, or persons, living or dead, is entirely coincidental and beyond the intent of the author or the publisher. No part of this book may be reproduced in any form or by any electronic or mechanical means, including photocopying, recording, information storage and retrieval systems, without written permission from the author, except for the use of brief quotations in a book review.

Copyright © 2020 by Charmaine Pauls

All rights reserved.

Photography by Wander Aguiar Photography LLC

Cover model Dina Auneau

Cover design by Okay Creations

ISBN: 978-2-491833-02-2 (eBook)

ISBN: 979-8-565858-08-2 (Print)

❦ Created with Vellum

CHAPTER 1

Maxime

*J*esus.
 I dive for the edge, going after Zoe over the cliff. The thought of losing her hurts my chest. It hurts a thousand times more than the cold water. When I hit the surface, I don't go down far. I turn and swim up like a madman. The sea is flat. I should easily spot her, but there are rocks all around. Shouting her name, I scout the water like a lunatic as a vise of fear closes around my heart.

Then I see her. Thank fuck. The relief is so great I'm not even angry. I swim with powerful strokes and reach her in five seconds. She's gasping and splashing, treading water. Grabbing her around the waist, I turn her onto her back and swim us to the shore. There's no way she could've made it out on her own, not knowing where the underwater rocks give way to form a channel.

I'm out of breath when we reach the beach, but not from exertion. It's the fear. I've never felt anything like it, never cared enough.

Dragging her out onto the sand, I put the revelation to the back of my mind to dissect later. I peel my jacket Zoe is still wearing off her body and cover her slender frame with my body, letting some of my heat warm her skin. Her teeth are chattering, and her limbs are shaking.

Fuck, fuck, fuck.

I lift her into my arms and start the steep ascent. The guards are waiting at the top, staring down with concerned faces, offering hands and assistance.

I brush them away. "We're fine."

Holding her close to my chest, I hurry to the bathroom where I run a shower. When the water is warm, I push her under the spray and undress her. Since I destroyed her underwear, she's wearing nothing but the red evening dress. Her lips are blue. So are her fingernails. I rub each of her hands between mine to warm them, and then her arms to aid the blood flow and increase her body temperature.

Somewhere between soaping her body and rinsing her hair, her teeth stop chattering. I brace her against the wall and drop to my knees in front of her. Droplets of water cling to her eyelashes as she stares at me, keeping her balance with her hands pressed on my shoulders. Her dark hair, normally wavy or curly, hangs straight and silky over her shoulders. Her breasts are big for her small body, her nipples a dark shade of pink. She doesn't shave or trim the triangle between her legs, but even there her hair is soft and perfect, a pretty womanly shape. There are many kinds of beautiful and plenty of norms to define it, but she's all of them, everything condensed into one.

Lifting her thigh, I hook it over my shoulder and worship her body with my hands. I circle her narrow waist and drag my palms over the curve of her hips, all the while watching her telltale eyes. They go hazy with need, the blue turning a shade darker, like the depths of the ocean. Her cheeks turn pink, and her nipples harden. I sweep a path down the outside of her legs and back up inside to her pussy. She's slick and swollen, her flesh needing what I've denied her earlier at the hotel.

I hold her eyes as I go down on her, eating her like she's my last meal. It doesn't take long for her to break. When she comes in my mouth, her long lashes brush her cheeks, and she catches her bottom lip between her teeth. I eat her out through the aftershocks of her orgasm, lapping up all her honey with lazy strokes of my tongue.

She's legless when I wrap her up in my robe and towel her dry. The exhaustion is a combination of my earlier punishing lesson, the sleepless night, the shock of what she's seen at Alexis's place, the afterglow of the orgasm, and coming down from the adrenaline of her goddamn jumping stunt. That's a lot for one small flower to take in all at once.

She doesn't protest when I carry her to my bed and pull the covers over us. I curl up with her back against my chest and her ass in my groin. I fold one arm under her head and the other around her waist. Like this, she's secure in the prison of my arms, finally warm and sated.

Kissing her neck, I inhale the sweet scent of her skin. "What the hell were you thinking, Zoe?"

"I wanted to know if I could do it," she says, her voice already thick with sleep.

"You could've fucking died."

"That would've been a bad thing?"

"Yes," I say vehemently. "You're never to do that again. Ever. Understand?"

"You did."

"I know what I'm doing."

"I did it, didn't I?"

I sigh. "You did, but there was no way you could've come out on the beach on your own. The rocks would've shredded you to pieces."

"Don't worry. I know why you're concerned." Her tone turns bitter. "It's this thing going on with Damian. Rest assured, I'm not going to kill myself."

Damn right, she isn't. Damn wrong, too. It's not just the *thing* with Damian. It's not about the diamonds or the business. It's about what I realized out there in those dangerous waters.

"Go to sleep," I say, tightening my arms around her.

She abides with a little sigh, her breathing soon evening out. Me, I lie awake, my heart thundering in my chest as I hold the woman who makes me feel, the only person in the world who makes me fear.

CHAPTER 2

Zoe

In the days that follow, Maxime behaves differently toward me. Sometimes, he worships me on his knees like he can never get enough of me, and at other times he pushes me away, deliberately keeping me at a distance. It's a never-ending push and pull. Through it all, he treats me well. As long as I'm sticking to my end of the bargain, he does. He's proving to me that he's good for his word, that he'll make my stay pleasant if I'm obedient, but he won't hesitate to punish me cruelly if I step out of line.

When I ask about the woman Alexis tortured, he only tells me she's fine. I ask about Alexis too, but Maxime says he's paid for what he's done and that's that. He refuses to divulge anything more. I know his family is wealthy. I've seen their properties and the lifestyles they live. Maxime told me they were powerful, but I didn't register exactly how much until now. Who gets away with what Alexis did? It's wrong. There's something disturbing about it, something significant, but there's already so much to deal with I block it out. Survival isn't only about the physical. It's also about the emotional and mental, and I'm processing as much as my mind can handle.

On a spring evening when Maxime seems to be in a good mood, I dare to bring up the subject that has been bothering me ever since the night he saved that woman from his brother. We're sitting on the couch in the library, me with a book in my hands and my feet in Maxime's lap. He's reading work related documents while massaging my feet.

"Maxime?"

He doesn't look up from the paper in his hand. "Mm?"

"Why wasn't Alexis convicted?"

He strokes a thumb along the curve of my sole. "Some punishments are better doled out by ourselves."

"You mean taking the law into your own hands."

Flicking over the page with one hand, he says, "Something like that."

I drop the book in my lap, no longer interested in the story. "Didn't the woman lay charges?"

"She didn't have to." Abandoning the massaging, he drags a palm over the bridge of my foot. "Alexis was punished, and she was compensated."

"She was okay with that?"

He lowers the papers. "Not with what happened, obviously, but she was satisfied that justice was done." His mouth tightens. "What's with all the questions? It's over. You should stop thinking about it."

"I just don't understand."

"What don't you understand?" he asks with impatience.

"How you could get away with something like that. Is it because your family is powerful? Because you have the right connections?"

He squeezes my foot. "Don't worry your pretty little head over that. As I said, you should forget that night happened."

"Just like that." I sit up straighter. "It's not something I'll ever be able to forget."

He sighs. "I regret taking you there. In hindsight, it was an error."

"Why did you?" When I try to pull my foot from his grasp, he holds tight.

"I've been asking myself the same thing." He stares at the empty fireplace. "I knew I'd need your help and that the woman was going to be more comfortable with the presence of another woman than more men descending on her, but I also wanted you to know who Alexis truly is."

"You took me there to see for myself."

He meets my eyes squarely. No remorse shines in his. "That was part of the reason, yes."

"Are you involved in worse crimes than kidnapping?"

His smile is cold. "What do you think?"

"What is it?" I pull my leg again, and this time he lets my foot go. "Drugs? Is that why you have all the guards around? I mean, the diamonds are legal if you buy them from Dalton's mine like you claimed, right?"

"You think too much."

"But—"

"No more."

The harsh tone shuts me up.

In a gentler voice, he continues, "No more speaking of this. Understand?"

Holding his gaze, I lift my chin. I hate how he keeps me in the dark. His look turns more predatory, lust bleeding into the gray pools that were flat and emotionless only a second ago as he grips my jaw in his big hand. Sexual awareness filters into the moment. The air becomes charged. With the innocent foot massage suddenly forgotten, I turn into prey. When he drags me closer, a tinge of fear mixes with anticipation. I do forget. I forget as long as he kisses me, and when he undresses me, we no longer speak.

THERE ARE many subjects Maxime doesn't like to discuss. We don't mention my jump, but I do feel better for it. Stronger. I did something scary and pushed my boundaries. It reinforced my spirit. It helps me keep my soul intact while I give my body to my captor on a daily basis. It helps me ignore that I come every time, that I crave his touch and sometimes his roughness. It helps me cope with who I've become.

No matter how I look at it, I can't see myself like Maxime wants me to. He claims he doesn't see me as a whore. That isn't real. It's make-believe, a fantasy he stole from my dream to enact in a castle on the edge of a cliff in France. He treats me like the princess I've always wanted to be, showering me with every possible material luxury, but it doesn't change the fact that I'm selling my body or being locked up in his tower.

However, he still allows me outside at free will, and I walk the grounds frequently, spending long hours looking out at the ocean. I walk in the gardens, the maze, and go down to the beach. It should be nice in summer. His guards never speak to me, not even when I greet them, but they do keep a close eye on me. If Maxime is home when I'm outside, I often see him standing on the terrace, watching me from afar, and from closer whenever I dare it near the cliffs again. I'm not going to jump a second time. Once was enough.

We go out often, eating in restaurants in town or visiting the sights. We walk around hand in hand like a couple in love while Maxime buys me treats at ice cream and strawberry stalls. He dresses and feeds me, and I say thank you with a smile. I don't like being the eye candy on his arm, but he insists the outings are good for me. Maybe they are. Maybe they keep me from going insane.

Francine comes in every weekday and every second weekend, but she avoids me. I keep out of the kitchen. I don't have any friends. I have no one to confide in. All I have are my letters to Damian, which I write faithfully every week.

A tutor arrives and I take up learning French. The course is intensive, four hours of classes a day plus two hours of homework. It's a good distraction for my mind. I've always enjoyed languages, and I'm a fast learner. It amuses Maxime to no end. He enjoys holding me on his lap in front of the fire in the evenings, making me repeat phrases and testing my vocabulary. He says my accent is adorable. It makes him smile. When I'm not working in the library with my tutor

—an elderly man Maxime no doubt appointed only because of his age—I'm doing homework in the tower. I've pulled the desk to the window, using the window seat as a chair, and now that the weather is changing it's not so cold up there.

My life takes on a routine, a predictable one that makes it easier to cope, and when the jasmine starts to bloom and poppies bleed all over the wild grass near the cliffs, I can hold a basic conversation in French and understand most of what's spoken. My reading isn't bad, either.

On a sunny afternoon when the birds are loud in the garden Maxime comes home with a big box. His granite eyes are unusually bright with excitement. He installs the box on the table in the dining room and takes my hand to pull me closer.

"For you," he says, watching me with eager attention.

"Me?" There's nothing printed on the outside, no clue as to what's inside.

"Open it."

I pull at the masking tape, but I don't manage to break the seal.

"Fran," he calls toward the kitchen. "Bring a pair of scissors."

We're still speaking English when we're together, a habit from when we met that stuck.

Francine enters with a pair of scissors, eyeing the box with curiosity.

"What is it?" I ask, taking the scissors. I can't help my smile. Maxime's excitement is contagious. I've never seen him like this before.

"A gift," he says.

"A gift?" Francine looks at him. "That's a first."

He shrugs. "Are you going to open it today, still?"

I laugh. "Maybe you should open it."

"I'm tempted, but that's not how it works with gifts." Stepping closer, he cups my cheek, giving me a look so tender the foundations of the fortress around my heart shake a little.

Remembering Francine is watching us, I step back to escape the intimate touch. "What?"

Maxime smiles, soft and genuine. "I like it when you laugh. I should buy you gifts more often."

"You do," I say. "All the time." I'm not going to tell him I still feel like the extravagant clothes and jewelry are payments for my obedience and payoffs for my body. I don't think I can handle a repeat of what I went through on the night of the auction.

"Those things are utile," he says. "It's not the same."

It makes me all the more curious. Attacking the box with the scissors, I make both of us laugh. It's easy and carefree. It's been a long time since I've laughed like this.

Finally, I manage to pry the edges of the box open and peer inside. It's filled with shredded paper. I glance at him.

"Go on," he says, waving me on.

I brush the paper aside and catch a glimpse of white metal. I still, then scoop the paper aside faster, making it fall over the table and floor.

Oh, my God. I lift the owner's manual from the box. A Singer Quantum Stylist computerized portable sewing machine.

I gape at him. "Maxime."

"Do you like it?" There's uncertainty in his tone.

Emotions clog up my throat. I've had only one true gift in my life—a book of fairytales. The clothes Maxime buys are to make me look pretty for him and to be a showpiece worth looking at on his arm. The flowers he bought in Venice were a pre-consolation price for locking me up in a cell. This? This is different. This is not for him or the benefit of outside onlookers. This isn't a prelude to a lesson. This is for me. This is the first thing he's given me with no strings attached. It serves no other purpose than making me happy. I don't know what makes me sadder, that he's the first person other than my late mom to gift me anything or that he's the only one who's paid enough attention to me to know what I love. No matter that I hate it, he understands my dreams. No matter that I hate myself for it, his gesture moves me. Tears well in my eyes, unbidden and unwelcome but very sincere as I digest the enormity of his offering.

He frowns. "What's wrong?"

He looks so dejected I can't stop myself from wrapping my arms around him and leaning my cheek on his chest. His gift is a beautiful gesture, a pure one, and I'm not going to twist it into something ugly by throwing it back into his face. It will kill any shred of kindness left in his dark heart, proving to him kind acts are rewarded with cruelty. I refuse to be the teacher of such an inhumane lesson.

"Thank you," I whisper, hugging him tightly.

He folds his arms around me. "You're welcome."

Francine stands stiffly with a downturned mouth. With all the emotions coursing through me, I've all but forgotten about her. We've shut her out in our private moment. When she catches my eye, she turns on her heel and heads back to the kitchen.

Maxime kisses the top of my head. "I didn't want to give it to you before you've finished your French exams. I was afraid you wouldn't focus."

He's right. I can hardly focus on anything other than the designs already running through my head. "I haven't written my exams yet." It's only in two days.

"Knowing what a nerd you are, I'm sure you've already mastered everything."

"Almost."

"You'll have to go shopping for fabric and thread and whatever else a clothing designer needs."

Sniffing away my tears, I pull back to look at him. "You mean a seamstress."

"No." He wipes a thumb under my eye, catching a tear. "I think you should go to a design school."

I stare at him. "What?"

"It's a good school, one of the most prestigious in the country right here in Marseille. I've already looked into it. You can start after the summer break."

I'm battling to process the information. "Don't you have to pass very strict tests to be admitted?" They only take the best of the best, and I know how selective places are.

"Of course, but I have no doubt you'll pass. I've seen your drawings."

"You think they have merit?"

He smiles. "Without a doubt."

Excitement surges through me, but confusion, too. "Why would you do something like that for me?" I also know how much designing schools cost. I can't even begin to think how much he'd have to fork out to send me to a prestigious French one.

"It's good to have a purpose in life. I don't believe in wasting talents. Hard work is rewarding. All the more if said work is your passion."

He wants me to have purpose, to live my passion? To make me happy or to prevent me from jumping off cliffs? I'm not clear about his motivations. I've never understood them. There's still so much I don't know about the man who both holds me captive and protects me from people like his brother. I know nothing about his passion or purpose.

"Do *you* live your passion?" I ask.

"I was born to do what I'm doing."

"Dealing in diamonds?" I don't even know if he's a broker or the owner of a jewelry chain.

"That's just a part of the business." Taking my hand, he says, "We'll unpack your sewing machine later. Walk with me to the beach."

I'm eager to please him, not because he gave me a gift or is willing to let me study at his expense, but because he showed me he's capable of true kindness, that not everything in his heart is dark.

We take the path, using the steep steps to climb down. I'm wearing a summer dress and sandals, even if the days are not yet warm. Maxime is still wearing his business suit. On the sandy part, the cliffs shelter us from the wind. Nevertheless, he removes his jacket and hangs it over my shoulders before taking off his shoes and socks. We sit down close to the edge of the water. The sun sparkles on the turquoise surface. A seagull calls from close by.

The smell of salt is stronger here, and the sun is warm on my back. It's nice. Peaceful. Pleasant. But the weather and the view aren't alone in creating this feeling of contentedness. It's sitting beside him in silent harmony. It's being something other than an object, someone with a purpose in life that doesn't revolve around my brother and Maxime's mysterious reasons for keeping me.

"What are you thinking?" he asks in his sensual accent.

I turn my face toward him. His features are as sharp and unattractive as the day we met, but after all these months, I look at him differently. There's a term for that. It's called sex appeal.

"Zoe?"

I look away from the face I shouldn't find handsome in the slightest, digging my fingers into the soft sand. "I was thinking about Damian."

He covers my hand with his. "What about him?"

"I miss him."

"He's doing fine. You don't have to worry about him."

I turn my head back to him quickly. "You have news?"

"I'm keeping tabs on him."

I frown. "You didn't tell me."

"It goes without saying, doesn't it?"

I search the gray depth of his eyes, the secrets he keeps from me. He still hasn't answered the question I posed on the night I jumped into the sea. "Why are you keeping me, Maxime? Why are you threatening me with Damian's life?"

His gaze turns flat. My heart sinks. He's not going to let me in.

Letting go of my hand, he drags his fingers through his hair. "Stop asking questions I can't answer."

"Can't or won't?"

He rises. "It's time to head back. I have work to do."

Not yet. I don't want this to end so soon. If there's one lesson captivity has taught me, it's to make the most of the good moments. You never know when there will be another one, if ever.

Reaching up, I close my fingers around his to hold him back. His eyebrows snap together as he looks at me. I think back to our picnic, to how he pushed me down onto the blanket in the open, and how it aroused me.

"Oh, my little flower." His voice is deeper, his gaze sharper. "You're taking a risk showing your lust so openly."

Yes, it must be showing on my face. I yearn for him to stretch and fill me. Pulling on his hand, I drag him back down beside me. Every time he takes me, I open up my body, making myself vulnerable, but he makes himself vulnerable, too. That's why he keeps on pushing me as hard as he's pulling. He's scared. Just like me. The revelation filters intuitively into my mind as our gazes remain locked in a heated stare.

This time it's me who shoves him down with my hands on his shoulders. His pupils widen. He resists a little, as if he's uncertain about submitting to me, but then lets me push him flat onto the sand.

I unbuckle his belt and pull down his zipper. He's hard already, his cock bulging in his underwear. I don't look up to see if there are guards on the perimeter of the cliff. I'm too scared to break our fragile eye contact, too afraid he'll reject me. This is different. He's always done the taking and set the rules. With the exception of the night of the auction, he's always taken care of my pleasure, but sex happens on his terms. Even the times I've craved release, he's given it by using the signals of my body to predict and fulfill my needs. I've never asked for it, not like this, and it's so damn scary because deep inside, in a hidden part of me, I hunger for more.

I crave affection.

True affection.

My body is sated, but my heart is so empty. I have no one else to turn to but him. He's made sure of that. He's the only man who can give me anything as long as I'm locked up in his house and he owns my life.

"Maxime." His name is a broken whisper.

Until this moment, I never would've clutched this knife of hope in my hands, ready to shred my own heart with the betrayal of my emotions, but he showed me kindness. He put that knife in my hands when he gave me hope. The rest is science. I've been open and vulnerable for too long. I'm a receptive reservoir. I'm a romantic. It's just who I am. I'm desperate for a few crumbs of affection. He wants my body, but I want to mean more.

I want to be more than a whore and a pawn.

It's the biggest risk I've taken, freeing his cock. Straddling him, I press a kiss to the tip. He leans back on his arms, watching me with wary attention. I grip the base in one hand. He's so hard, so much man. He shudders when I lick the underside, and when I take him to the back of my throat he surrenders. Something inside me gives as he folds his arms under his head in the sand, his guard relaxing. I reward him by sucking him the way he likes, the way he taught me. He groans, lifting his hips a fraction, but he maintains his position of immobility, allowing me to choose.

I do. I choose to move my underwear aside and lower myself over his hard length. With every inch I take him deeper, I let the cold, hurtful blade of hope into my heart. I moan at how completely he fills me, at the bite of pain that comes with the stretch. My fingers clench in the fabric of his shirt, his jacket falling over us like a cloak when I lean forward and slide my body up and down. The pleasure is exquisite. Hard. Dark. I whimper as our groins press together. The angle is just right, adding friction to my clit, but I need to see his face. I need to look into his eyes when I fall, hoping to God there will be just one small spark of warmth for me.

Leaning back, I brace my hands on his thighs and ride him. I hold onto his gaze as release starts winding through my body. His jaw is tight, his gray eyes gleaming. He's ablaze just as I am, but his flames only go skin deep. Still, I cling to the sharpness in those pools that cut into my soul. If he could only give me a drop, just a little to survive.

I rock faster, my sounds and thoughts already splintering as my climax builds. My cry is desperate. "Maxime, please."

Satisfaction bleeds into his eyes, sharpening his edges, making him seem crueler as he recognizes his power over me. "Please, what?"

The words spill over my lips, a request that leaves me utterly powerless. "Please, love me."

He freezes. A shutter falls over his eyes. In a blink, he switches off. *No.*

Tears burn at the back of my eyes. "Please," I whisper, "just a little."

A vein pulses in his temple. For a moment, we're stuck in a terrible limbo. It's a defining moment. It's the moment I fall for my captor, admitting I want—need—more from him than sex.

Just like that, the show is over. He moves from spectator to orchestrator. Grabbing my upper arms, he flips us around. I'm pinned in the sand by his heavy body and hard cock. The fever in his eyes is new. Cold. Buttons fly as he rips open the bodice of my dress. He flips the cups of my bra down, exposing my breasts. His fingers are punishing on my nipples, twisting and pinching. He pulls out and slams into me as if he's trying to break me in two.

The breath leaves my lungs with every thrust. Tears leak from the corners of my eyes. I hold onto his shoulders as he pivots his hips with a furious tempo, eradicating any earlier softness. It's animalistic and carnal. It's us. I was stupid to think it could ever be different. Stupid to want things I can never have. I should've known better, but now it's too late.

I climax with a raw cry, my body and heart falling apart as he rips his cock from me and comes over my breasts. His breathing is ragged and his expression wild. The birth control is long since effective, but he's still using a condom. And now, he didn't come inside me.

Shame surges through me. He humiliated me. On purpose. Another lesson. He'll never have feelings for me. I can blame it all on him, but I've also humiliated myself by opening up to him. The pain is brilliant. It slices me up with cruel, precise cuts. I can't stand for him to see me like this—something used and discarded. Gripping the shredded fabric of my dress, I cover my breasts.

"Zoe."

I lift my gaze to his. For the first time since I've known him, he's at a loss for words. Whatever is going through his mind, I don't want to hear it.

"Please," I say, "don't say anything."

Indecision plays over his features as he scans my face. Then he leans in and kisses me. The kiss is violent. I make a protesting sound, trying to turn my head away, but he catches my face in his hand. His fingers hurt my jaw. His teeth cut my tongue. I relent, going slack in his hold. At least like this, we don't have to talk.

He only lets me breathe when stars explode behind my eyes. I can't meet his gaze any longer. I'm looking at the sun from over his shoulder, letting the bright rays blind me.

"I'm sorry," he says, sitting up with his knees straddling my hips.

I laugh. "For what?"

"For spoiling your moment. I shouldn't have taken over."

I shrug, sinking a little deeper into the sand. "It wasn't my moment."

Tilting his head toward the sky, he scrubs a hand over his face. He opens his mouth, closes it again, and finally says, "If it's any consolation, I've never said sorry to anyone before."

"Okay." I close my eyes, seeing red spots from the sun.

I could be on an island, a castaway, trying to survive alone. It'll be an exciting game, a loveless dream in which to escape, but dreaming is no longer my escape. I think I've lost the ability altogether.

His sigh caresses my ears. I open my eyes when he buttons his jacket up over my torn dress and adjust his clothes. Getting to his feet, he offers me a hand.

I don't accept it. I stand on my own.

I did something despicable. I fell for my kidnapper in a yearning need for affection. I opened my heart, and I did it willingly. I exposed myself to his rejection and took it like a punch in the chest.

I may have lost this bet, but I'm still standing.

From now on, it's me on my own.

CHAPTER 3

Maxime

Zoe wants love. I'll give her anything in my power, except for letting her go, but love is the one thing I can't give. I'm not capable of loving. I care for her more than anyone. She makes me terrified that anything should happen to her, for fuck's sake. I've long since dissected my fear and categorized it. I fear because I care. I've accepted it. But love? That's a step I don't know how to take.

I stole her because I wanted her hope. I wanted her secrets. I thought if I could figure out how she could survive her dysfunctional family in her disadvantaged neighborhood and still shine like a light in the dark, maybe so could I. I took her for purely selfish reasons, because I saw her as my ticket to happiness. My little experiment, but then, she became my own little wildflower in a vase, and I no longer wanted to let her go.

Of course, keeping her here is detrimental to our plan to guarantee her brother supplies us with diamonds when he takes back his mine. To my family, she's our pawn. To me, that's just a bonus. I promised my father I'd make sure she'd want to stay. I've planned everything so carefully, how I was going to make her happy. I gave her every clue she scattered around in her apartment that pointed to a dream—the trip to Venice, more pretty clothes than she can ever need, and a place in an elitist fashion design school. Yet I've forgotten about this crucial little detail. Love. Love features so lowly in my spectrum of feelings, I sometimes forget it exists. What did I expect? Of course, Zoe wants love. She's a romantic. A dreamer. Above all, she deserves love. Maybe if she learns to love me she can love enough for the both of us.

My thoughts are dark as I head to my father's office in the morning. I'm berating myself for my slipup, for overlooking such an important factor in my shrewd plan to keep her. One thing is for sure. I'm not planning on sending her back to her brother. Ever.

She's mine.

Mulling over this new development, I walk into the office. My father is already behind his desk, even if it's earlier than his usual arrival time. Alexis stands by the coffee machine. He doesn't look at me as I enter, but the paper cup dents in his hand. We don't speak about what happened in the warehouse. I practically left him and his buddy for dead. It took him more than a couple of weeks to recover. I have no idea if his buddy survived. All I know is he's no longer around. He's either six feet under or he bailed. My father knows about the lashing, but not about the rest. I left the details up to Alexis to share, and it seems he's too proud to let anyone else know his fat friend came twice in his ass. He hasn't touched a prostitute since. Point taken. Lesson learned. I'd say the unfortunate event was successful. I grin as I pour my coffee, taking pleasure from how Alexis's jaw snaps tighter.

The toilet in the adjoining bathroom flushes. The door opens, and Leonardo steps out. I tense. What the fuck is the Italian doing here? Since my father is watching me closely, I don my poker face.

"Max." Leonardo walks over, his eyes scanning my face like a shark. "How are you? We don't see much of you in the club."

I raise a brow. "I didn't know you were frequenting the club."

"I've been over on a few weekends." He rolls his shoulders. "You know, to get a feel for the territory."

"So you've said." Sitting down, I leave my coffee on the desk and steep my fingers together.

"We have a situation." My father indicates the free chairs facing his desk.

Leonardo and Alexis each takes a seat.

"The *Brise de Mer* is sending more men to Marseille," my father continues. "Their number has doubled in one week."

I tap my fingers on the desk. "Under what guise?"

My father's voice is gravelly, a sign of his irritation. "An annual gathering."

Alexis moves to the edge of his seat. "Let me take out a few of those Corsican fuckers. That should send a message."

"No," I say. My brother has always been too bloodthirsty, just like my father. "That'll start a war."

"Maybe that's what they want," Leonardo says.

My reply is sharp. "Then they can start it. We'll fight, and we'll win, but we sure as hell won't take responsibility for a bloodbath." That'll put us in the bad books of our government supporters. As long as we play by the rules, no one will blame us for defending ourselves.

"What do you suggest?" Alexis asks. "That we sit on our asses and do fucking nothing while they invade our territory?"

I give him an easy smile that only infuriates him more. "That we give them the benefit of the doubt."

My father's chair protests with a squeak as he leans back. "It's too soon to make a move, but I want our men to keep tight tabs on these motherfuckers. There's no way they're taking back Marseille."

"We've kicked them out once," Leonardo says. "We'll kick them out again."

The *we* grates on my nerves. The young fuck is already taking credit for a history that has nothing to do with him, for blood that never soiled his hands. I, however, know why my father wants him here. We're using the legal money from our diamond business to sponsor the illegal activities, and we're constantly looking for new ways of laundering that money.

The second reason why my father wants him here is the real thorn in my side. It's not a done deal yet, but soon I'll have to take Leonardo under my wing and treat him like a protégé. One, I work alone, even if I still answer partially to my father, and two, Leonardo is clever. He's already seen what's important to me. He's ambitious. He's not going to be content with tagging along in my shadow forever. At some stage, he's going to want to climb the ladder, and he'll use any weakness he can exploit against me. Meaning Zoe, the beautiful woman I can't let go.

"Agreed." My father slams a hand on the desk to indicate the meeting is over.

When Alexis and Leonardo get to their feet, he motions for me to stay. Alexis shoots me a hateful glare on the way to the door. I catch the way he locks eyes with my father before he leaves. I often think Raphael is disappointed that I'm the first-born who inherited the power instead of his favorite son.

My father waits until the door closes before speaking. "You haven't been home for months."

"I've been busy."

His fixes me with his droopy-eye stare. "Your mother misses you."

"She could come over."

His hand curls into a fist on the table. "She won't as long as you're keeping that woman in your house."

"Her name is Zoe."

He clenches his jaw. "I know what her name is."

I lean forward. "Then use it."

His smile is slow to come, his patience forced. "Family comes first."

"Yes, a point you're proving well."

He narrows his eyes. "You better watch your tone with me, son."

My smile matches his. "No disrespect intended. Just stating the facts."

"You've taken this game far enough."

One by one, my muscles lock. "What's that supposed to mean?"

"She compromises everything—the Italian connection, our family. It will be in everyone's best interest to hand her over to Alexis as agreed. He's learned his lesson. He won't make such a mistake again."

The last part makes my body coil like a predator preparing for an attack. My voice is even, betraying nothing of the fury running under the surface. "I won't let her come between business or the family. It's working fine as it is." This discussion is over. To prove it, I get up. "Anything else?"

"No." My father's tone is cold. "Not for now." As I turn, he says, "Go visit your mother." I'm already across the floor when he calls after me, "You're breaking her heart."

I slam the door on my way out. It's true that I've been avoiding my parents' home after the way the women treated Zoe, but I'm not insensitive to their point of view. I know it's hard for Maman. I'm not behaving like the good, Catholic son she raised. In her eyes, I'm acting more like my father.

When I've done the round at the docks and poured over the books, I head out to the house of my childhood. It's been more or less a happy childhood, with Maman always fussing over me and Father being absent for most of my younger years. It's only when I entered high school that he started involving me in the business, trying to forge a bond that was never there to start from the beginning. In a way, he resented me for how Maman babied me, and Maman lavished me with attention because she had no one else.

I park out front and go through the house. The housekeeper—a new girl whose name I can never remember—tells me Maman is out back. I find her in a deckchair on the terrace with a book.

She puts the book aside when she sees me. "Max."

I bend down to kiss her cheeks. "How are you?"

She waves a hand. "As you can see."

I sit down in the chair. It's not her fault that she's lonely. She has always looked out for me. I shouldn't forget that. "I've been busy."

Her mouth puckers. "Too busy for your family?"

"You know why I didn't come."

"Because you can't bring *her*?"

I sigh. "She was a guest, Maman. I expected better from you."

"You thought it was all right to flaunt your lover around for all your family to see, to gloat over, gossip about, and point fingers at me?"

"Why would anyone point fingers at you?"

She sits up straighter. "For failing in my job to raise you well."

"This has nothing to do with raising me well."

Her voice takes on a pleading tone. "Max, what you're doing isn't right."

"Maman, stop it. We've been through this."

She falls back against the cushions. "I never thought I'd say this, but you're your father's son, after all."

I smile. "Emotional blackmail won't work with me. You can drop the act."

She takes my hand. "If you must, then do it, but get her out of your system and fast. This can't end well for either of you."

Squeezing her fingers, I stand. I owe my mother much, but Zoe isn't negotiable. "I'm sure you'll like her if you give her a chance."

Her expression is pained. "How can you even expect such a thing from me? My loyalty is with the family. *Our* family."

She's right, of course. What I've been asking is impossible. "I'm sorry for putting you in a difficult position. It was selfish of me."

Her face softens. "Get this girl out of your system and send her home."

My smile is grim. If only it was that simple.

"Come over for lunch on Sunday. I'll invite your cousins."

I hesitate. A few months ago, I never would've declined a family lunch. Now I can't make peace with leaving Zoe on her own. It wouldn't be fair to her, either. "We'll see."

My mother's face falls.

Kissing her forehead, I say goodbye and break every speed limit to get home to my mistress as my mother's words repeat in my head. I can no longer deny that I'm gambling with both of our futures—Zoe's and mine. But where there's a will there's a way, and if anyone has a will where she's concerned, it's me.

CHAPTER 4

Zoe

After Maxime's rejection that day on the beach, he becomes even more invested in me. He's making up for the affection he can't give with lavish attention. We visit the theatre and swim in the cove when spring turns to summer. Sometimes, he reads to me in the garden on a picnic blanket with his head resting in my lap. He rubs my body with suntan lotion, worried my pale skin will burn, and helps me with my French exercises. I still do them, even if I've passed my exam. I like keeping my mind busy.

My body is constantly sore from being used, the ache between my legs never preventing me from wanting him. He's all I have. Sometimes I think this can be enough, but sometimes, when I sit alone with a book in the tower, I long for someone to love me, someone to need me for more than my body. The more attention Maxime lavishes on me, the more my insecurity grows. Beauty is a feeble currency. It doesn't last forever. Bodies grow old. How long before he goes hunting for the next woman, someone younger and fresher, someone less used than me?

The day will come when he'll discard me—four years, give or take, from now—and by then there will be nothing left of my soul. He would've devoured it all. Everyday, I'm losing a little more of myself to him. The hole in my heart, the one I've cut myself with my stupid yearning for love, is tearing wider with each passing day. I can't stop it. I can't help the feelings filtering in, the treacherous loving Maxime only feeds with his twisted kindness and devotion.

The summers here are as unforgiving as the wet winters with its icy winds. It gets so hot most days I feel wilted, but the old house is fresh inside and sometimes there's a breeze from the sea that cools the air down. On those days, we have dinner prepared by a grumpy Francine on the terrace.

I work hard on my designs during summer and have a collection ready when the school submissions open in July. I'm nervous until August, much to Maxime's amusement, who says he finds my enthusiasm endearing. When the results finally come, Maxime calls me downstairs for dinner. The table in the garden under the old pine tree is set with a white tablecloth and a silver candelabra. It's a windless evening with no breeze to blow out the candles.

I eye the crystal flutes and the champagne in the ice bucket. "What's going on?"

"We have something to celebrate."

My chest expands. My cheeks heat in a rush of excitement. "We do?"

He pours two glasses and offers me one. "Congratulations."

I clutch the stem so hard I fear it may snap. "Really? I'm in?"

"I told you." He kisses my lips. "I never had a doubt."

"Oh, my God." I slam a hand over my mouth. "I can't believe it."

"To you," he says, raising his glass.

I watch him from under my lashes. "Thank you."

His voice turns husky. "Don't look at me like that."

"Like how?" I bite my lip.

The cold color of his eyes darkens to a stormy gray. "Like you want it rough."

He knows I do. I've never asked again, nor taken, not after the beach, but he's good at reading my body language. He's a master at predicting my needs.

Taking the glass from my hand, he places it with his on the table. Drops of condensation run in rivulets over the two glasses that stand side by side in the setting sun.

"Everyone out," he barks out in French.

The guards scatter, disappearing to wherever. For a rare moment we're alone in the garden and our exchange unobserved.

"Francine can—" I was going to say come out any minute, but Maxime has already fastened his hands around my waist and lifted me onto the table.

Impatiently, he pushes the candelabra away. His rugged features are heated and his concentration one-track minded as he sweeps his palms under my dress and up my inner thighs. I shiver when he reaches my sex. My underwear is already wet. Holding my eyes, he pushes the elastic aside and shoves three fingers inside. I like it when he's tender and gentle, but this is what I love. I love it when he doesn't prepare me, when the friction is unbearable and the stretch too much, when I can lose myself in the sensations and fall into the oblivion of ecstasy.

He rests his thumb on my clit and curls his fingers inside. He doesn't play with my clit. He just keeps his touch there. It drives me insane. I need more. He knows. Bracing my body with a palm on my lower back, he brings his lips to my nipple. When he sucks it through the fabric of my bra and dress, I arch against him, shamelessly surrendering to the pleasure he offers. I moan as he grazes the hard tip with his teeth. My nipples are sensitive. Just sucking on them is enough to bring me close to orgasm. He knows my body inside out. He knows what makes me beg and scream.

I know what he likes too. I cup his length while he twirls a tongue around my nipple, teasing me through too many layers of clothes.

When I squeeze, he leans into my palm. My favorite way of feeling him is outlining the shape of the broad head with a finger. The light caress drives him crazy. With a growl, he rips his fingers from my body and brushes my hand away to center his cock between my legs. His hard length rubs over my clit, pushing the wet fabric of my panties over the bundle of nerves, but it's not the silk I want to feel on my skin.

Digging my hands into the lapels of his jacket, I pull him to my mouth and take the kiss I want. He never denies me. He kisses me back with abandon and skill, making my body melt against his as all my nerve endings hum in need. I reach for his belt, fumbling with the buckle. He rips away my underwear. I'm starving, moaning as I pull down his zipper and sighing into his mouth when I finally fold my fingers around his cock. I stroke twice before catching the pre-cum on the tip and letting it lubricate my palm. It's the firm downward slide of my hand that makes him lose control. His groan is guttural as he grabs my wrist and forces my upper body down. My free hand is in his hair, pulling at the silky strands, holding his lips to mine, but he easily catches that one too, pinning both wrists in one hand above my head. He grips the base of his cock and guides it to my entrance. I brace myself, but never enough.

When he enters me fully with a single thrust, my body shifts up the table. He fastens a hand on my hip to hold me in place, pulls almost all the way out, and slams back. My back arches from the intense stimulation. It's more than I can take, but I lift my hips when he lowers his, meeting every thrust.

"Goddamn, Zoe."

His eyes are glittering darkly, hard granite cut from a rocky cliff. The candlelight plays over his face, the shadows making the hollows of his cheekbones deeper and the harsh lines of his nose and jaw starker. I long to trace the bump on the bridge of his nose, but when I test his hold he doesn't let go.

Kissing a path up my neck, he presses feverish words against my ear. "Do you know how beautiful you are?"

I still. The words trigger my suppressed insecurity, things I shouldn't and don't want to think about, but I can't stop myself from saying, "Not forever."

He slows his pace and lifts his head to look at me. "You'll always be beautiful."

"Not when I'm old."

"Then as much as now."

"Don't lie to me."

The lines around his eyes tighten. "I'm not lying to you."

"Just withholding the truth?"

"You need to know what you must. That's enough."

"Then tell me honestly, when will you tire of me?"

He stills completely. His expression becomes veiled. "You don't want me to answer that."

My passion turns to rage. The embers of everything adrift in my chest have caught fire, and the fear I've been pushing away for the last few months jumps into flames of fury. "When the next woman you can abduct comes along?"

His jaw bunches. "I'm not interested in other women."

"Only in whatever the hell you want from Damian?"

"No, my flower." Despite his clipped tone, his voice is soft. "I like to see the world through your eyes."

The answer is not what I expected. "Why?"

"You're everything I'm not."

I'm not sure what that means. It's strange to have this argument with my wrists pinned above my head and his cock buried deep in my body. I don't even know why or how the fight started, only that I can't finish this.

I pull on his hold. "Let me go."

His nostrils flare. "You're five seconds from coming and you want me to let you go?"

"That's what I said."

His smile is one I both fear and hate, a cruel one. "As you wish."

I'm empty when he pulls out of me, so incredibly cold that I fold my arms around my stomach. He flicks my skirt up over my hips and takes his cock in his hand. It only takes a few pumps before he comes, ejaculating thick streams of cum over my sex and my thighs.

When he's finished, he takes a napkin and cleans himself. Dumping the crumpled napkin on the table, he adjusts his clothes. "It seems you'll be happier with your own company tonight. As it's supposed to be a celebration, I won't spoil it for you."

The venomous words are hardly out before he turns and walks back into the house. I cover myself with shaky hands, pulling my dress down over my sticky thighs. My legs are wobbly when I push off the table. The setting is in disarray with the tablecloth full of folds and the crockery pulled askew. It's the remains of a wasted evening, the bitter result when feelings get in the way.

Francine exits with a tray. She places a platter on the table, but I'm too distraught to pay attention.

"Dinner for one?" she asks with a chuckle.

I stare at her face. Since when has this turned into a war between us? I suppose since the minute I set foot into this house.

"You're an unthankful bitch," she says, straightening the tablecloth.

"Excuse me?"

"This house, Maxime's protection, the gifts…Do you know how lucky you are?"

"I didn't ask for any of this."

"Most women will give anything for what you have, but don't worry." She winks. "You won't have to live here forever."

"What's that supposed to mean?"

Tilting her head, she gives me a smug smile. "Enjoy your meal."

I stare at her back until she disappears through the kitchen door. A part of me wants to go after Maxime. Another part wants to never see him again. That part is a lie. No matter how much I hate this inequality between us—the fact that I can't express myself freely and am only treated kindly when I behave—it's too late for me. I've formed a bond with Maxime. The fact that it's forced doesn't make the attachment weaker. If anything, it's stronger. He made me dependent on him in every sense—materially, physically, and emotionally. There's nowhere else to turn to. There's only this house now, this beautiful place I both love and hate, and him. Love and hate. That's an accurate description for what we share.

Taking the bottle of champagne, I kick my sandals off and make my way down to the beach. The sun is setting when I flop down in the sand, letting the water wash over my feet. It must be just after nine. By now it'll be pitch black, dark in South Africa. It took me a while to get used to the longer days. Some days are just too damn long. Tipping back the bottle, I swallow a mouthful. The champagne is deliciously dry. I finish half the bottle before my spirit is gratifyingly numbed.

It's so hot out here. Even at this hour, it's still over thirty degrees Celsius. Pushing to my feet, I fumble with the zipper of my dress. I stumble a little as I step out of the dress and unclasp my bra. Oh, dear. I think my torn underwear is still lying somewhere under the table. I better pick it up before the poor gardener finds it.

The water is clear and cool. I walk in until it reaches my waist, flinching as the salt burns the abused skin between my legs. I take another swig of the champagne and make a face. Yuk. It's lukewarm now.

After downing what's left in one go, I fling the bottle out on the sand and wade deeper into the water until I can drift on my back. The lights of the house on the cliff are blurry in my view. It forms a hazy picture as I try to fit the puzzle pieces of tonight together, of what Maxime said. No, wait. What Francine said. Oh, crap. Whatever. I think I'm a little drunk.

I'm such an idiot.

"Why's that, my little flower?" a husky voice asks.

Maxime? He's not supposed to be here. He should be upstairs in his big house, ruling over cliffs and kingdoms of diamonds with his iron fist.

"For falling for you," I reply.

Strong arms fold around me from behind, pulling me against a hard body. An impressive erection presses against my back. "I didn't give you a choice."

My words slur a bit. "What are you doing?"

"Making sure you don't drown."

"No," I say, wiggling when he slips his cock between my legs. "I mean what are you *doing*?"

Big hands cup my hips. Soft lips press on my shoulder and a warm breath washes over my neck. "Shh. I'm just going to make you come."

The broad head of his cock rubs over my clit before dragging through my folds. I want to ask why. I want to make sense of it all but then that hardness presses against my forbidden opening. I go still.

"Relax." He breathes against my ear.

Even in my drunken state, I can feel his dark excitement in the way his fingers tighten on my hips. I can hear it in the raw note of his voice. It stokes my fire. I've only had a taste of it once, and it hurt. I'm not sure I'm going to like it.

"You will," he says. "I'll make sure."

I said that out loud? Oh, God. I'm a lot drunker than I thought.

A burning sensation explodes in my dark entrance as he pushes through the tight ring of muscle. I cry out, trying to scoot away, but his fingers are on my clit, rubbing the way I like.

"Wrap your legs around me," he says.

The pleasure makes me blindly obedient, just the way he always wants me. I open my legs wider and hook my ankles around his thighs. My toes brush over sand. He's sitting on his heels with my back against his chest. We're shallow. He must've steered us closer to the shore.

I let my head fall on his shoulder. The act pushes out my breasts. I'm spread open. My body is a sacrifice, every hole accessible for his use. One hand finds my breast, gently rolling my nipple, while the other plays with my clit. I suck in a breath when he pushes his cock deeper. He holds still, letting me adjust. It still hurts, but I don't want him to stop. I want him to push me to my limits. I want to fly over the edge.

As he pushes two fingers inside my pussy, his cock slips deeper into my asshole. He curls his fingers inside and rolls his thumb over my clit until I'm soft and pliant enough to take all of him. This is nothing like the night at the hotel. This is twisted lust, not punishment. It's dark, and scary, and strangely exhilarating. He groans when I push back, a lustful sound that spurs me on. I lift higher and slide down over his length, focusing on the magic work of his fingers and how everything seems so full, stretched so tightly.

The pain is like a hot branding iron, but pleasure surfaces through the fire, sending mixed signals to my brain. I can't distinguish any longer. I can only feel the pleasure coiling around my insides, squeezing until my breath is gone.

"Breathe," he says, locking his fingers around the column of my neck.

I drag in a ragged breath, and then come so hard my teeth chatter. He doesn't let me go. He continues to massage my oversensitive clit, milking every ounce I have left until his cock grows even thicker and he yanks me to his body so hard I'll have bruises on my neck and hip tomorrow. He punches his hips up, even if he's already sheathed to the hilt. He thrusts twice more, grunting as he empties himself in my ass. It must be the singular most powerful orgasm of my life.

"You did beautifully," he whispers, "like I knew you would."

It burns when he pulls out. My body sags in his arms. He catches me around the shoulders and under my legs, holding me to his chest. Out of nowhere, right in the middle of my drunken state, the reason why I was so upset earlier hits me. I've fallen for him, and since he's incapable of returning my feelings I have no reassurance he won't replace me with someone else. Wait. Shouldn't I want him to replace me? Am I not supposed to want to get away? Isn't being his captive the reason for my anguish and unhappiness?

I don't know how I get back to the bedroom. Somewhere between the burn and gentle kisses I black out. My dream is weightless and painless, a place where broken hearts and bodies don't exist. Idle words float in and out on a moonlight breeze, words that bring both terror and salvation as they promise to never let me go.

CHAPTER 5

Zoe

There are nine girls in Madame Page's class at the Marseille-Mediterranean College of Art. Smelling of cigarette smoke, she's an elderly woman with red hair and overlarge, square-rimmed glasses.

A delicate girl with jet black hair and slanted eyes sits next to me.

"Hi," I say, taking my sketchpad from my satchel. "I'm Zoe."

She gives me a sidelong glance, then moves an inch toward her side of the drafting table. Lifting her chin, she says, "I'm Christine."

The woman on the other side of me snickers. She has dark brown hair and eyes, and freckles like mine. "I suppose you want to know my name, too," she says. "I'm Thérèse."

Madame Page walks into the center of the room. She's wearing a straight white dress with square pockets and black piping. It's a Saint Laurent number.

"Quiet, please. For your first lesson, I want to get a sense of each of your unique styles." She claps her hands together. "Quick now. Open your manual on module one."

I take out my notepad and pens while the others open the module on their laptops or tablets. Maxime won't allow me a laptop or tablet. I didn't even have the concession when I was studying French.

Madame Page pushes a printout titled Module One over the table without looking at me.

"Thank you," I say, accepting the stack of papers stapled together.

Going through the introductory module, Madame Page explains we'll start with the basics such as design principles, drawing, building form, textile science, business practices, and history, and work our way up to pattern creation. Practical design will only start in the second year for those who make it. A panel of independent judges will judge a design contest at the end of the second year, including compulsory evening wear and a wedding dress, to determine which scholars will make it to the third and final year. The competition is severe. Only six of us will be accepted into next year's level. She talks about perseverance and discipline before pointing out a few class rules. No eating and drinking. No chitchatting. No copycatting.

"I'm looking for a fresh perspective, for a unique style," she says. "Each of you shows potential." She locks eyes with Thérèse. "Thérèse, you have an eye for lines but you're lacking detail. In this class, we're going to work on your strengths and weaknesses." Skimming over me, she moves to Christine. "Christine, I love your dare, but there's a fine line between eccentric and flamboyance. Juliette, your simplicity is refreshing. I love how you play with color and texture. I'm looking forward to seeing more of your work."

One by one, she goes around the table, ignoring me. I shake it off. It was probably just an innocent oversight.

For the next hour, we make rough sketches and notes. Madame Page gathers the sketches and goes through our notes. She gives detailed feedback on each one with praise and critique, but she only glances at mine without making any comments.

My chest pulls tight as she places my pad back on the table. I flip the page back to find nothing written in red, not like on Thérèse and Christine's sketches.

"I bid you a good day, ladies," she says. "I'll see you tomorrow."

Taking my time to gather my stationary, I wait until everyone has left before approaching her worktable. "Madame Page?"

She looks up with a pinched expression. "Yes?"

"Is there a problem with my work?"

She goes back to what she was writing. "No."

I'm tempted to just leave, but this is too important to me. "I'm sorry, but I don't understand. Why didn't you critique my work?"

Her pencil makes a scratching sound as she pulls it over the paper. "You don't need my input, Mademoiselle Hart. You'll pass with flying colors."

The words don't elicit the warmth of pride in my chest. Instead, they leave me cold, a terrible notion making me shrivel. "You don't think I merit to be here, do you?"

"If that's all, I have work to do." She waves me off, not bothering to grace me with another glance.

Clutching my satchel under my arm, I make my way into the warm sunlight while coldness creeps over every inch of my skin. Maxime waits across the road, leaning on his fancy sports car. His eyes are trained on me, following my progress with undivided attention. Giving me this much freedom is a big deal for him, but I can't appreciate it. Not right now.

A few of the women from my class are gathered on the lawn in front of the building. They're looking my way, whispering as they too follow my progress toward the blue Bugatti.

I block them out. I block everything out. When Maxime kisses my lips, I can't help but pull back. He stills. The coldness I feel in my bones settles over his eyes, turning the gray to winter instead of molten skies.

"How was the first day?" he asks, his observation sharpening on me as he gets my door.

I don't bother to answer. There's a tick to his jaw, but I can't even bring myself to be scared. I just feel numb like on the night that was supposed to be a celebration when I drank myself into a stupor and spent the next day being sick. That sickness descends on me now, turning my stomach.

He says nothing as he starts the engine. The powerful hum of the motor is the only sound in my ears as he heads toward town.

When he doesn't take our exit, I snap out of my haze. "Where are we going?"

"To celebrate."

My stomach clenches. I dig my nails into my palms.

"We're having dinner in town." He glances at me. "There's an opening of a new casino."

"You have to be there," I say in a flat tone.

He changes gears and accelerates too abruptly. "Yes, but it'll still be a celebration."

I register his fancy suit and tie. "I'm not dressed for a party."

"I have a dress for you in the trunk."

I can't face one of his fancy affairs. Not today. "Maxime, please. I just want to go home."

His eyebrows pull together. "What's wrong?"

I'm suddenly so tired I sag in my seat. "I don't want to be your eye candy tonight."

His knuckles turn white on the gearstick. "Is it so terrible to be seen with me? Is that what was going on back there? You're happy enough for my money to pay for your classes, but you don't want your friends to know who's paying?"

They're not my friends. He made sure they'd never be. Rubbing a hand over my forehead, I say quietly, "They already know."

He brings the car to a screeching halt in front of a white building with a water fountain. Grabbing my jaw in his hand, he squeezes painfully. "You're mine, Zoe, for the whole fucking world to see. Is that clear enough, or is it time for another lesson?"

Tears gather in my eyes. I shake my head. "Please, Maxime. I can't do this. Not tonight. Just take me home."

He lets go, the momentum shoving me against the door. "You will go inside and get changed. You will wait for me in the room until I come and fetch you." His expression hardens. "How tonight turns out is up to you."

He gets out, comes around, and opens my door. Gautier and Benoit must've followed behind us. They get out of a Mercedes. Gautier takes a dry-cleaning and overnight bag from the trunk of Maxime's car. Benoit scans the entrance of the casino and steps aside for me to enter. I'm halfway across the pavement when Maxime catches my wrist.

"You forgot something." Yanking me against him, he cups my nape and kisses me.

The kiss is hot and intense, but I'm not in it.

Maxime tears his lips from mine and pushes me aside. "Make sure you're ready in an hour."

I walk on wooden legs to the door, following Gautier and Benoit through the lobby to an elevator. Gautier pushes the button for the top floor. Always the penthouse. He leaves the bags on the bed and checks the suite before locking me in.

I stand awkwardly in the middle of the floor, the lights of Marseille stretching out below like a bed of diamonds. The ache in my heart bleeds and grows. The shame and betrayal are like stains on my soul. I can almost forgive Maxime for making me fall in love with him. Almost. At least that wasn't intentional. It happened all on my part because I opened my stupid heart when I opened my body, but this I can never forgive.

Rushing to the telephone, I lift the earpiece and dial zero.

"Good evening, Miss Hart," a male voice says. "How may I assist you?"

"I'd like to make a local call, please." If I can reach the embassy, I can ask for help. "Can you connect me?"

He clears his throat. "Sorry, ma'am. No calls. Mr. Belshaw's instructions."

Of course. It was worth a try. "Thank you, anyway," I say before hanging up.

My gaze falls on the bottle of champagne cooling in the ice bucket, the cork already popped. I pour a glass, but stop before bringing it to my lips. I said I wouldn't become my father. Drowning my problems isn't going to help. I leave the glass on the table and unzip the bag on the bed. It's a pink dress—simply beautiful. Silk rose petals are sewn onto the skirt with teardrop crystals. I brush my fingers over the stretch velvet fabric, admiring the craftsmanship. The dress looks as if it's made from rose petals that are scattered with drops of dew. It must've taken hours to hand-sew the detail. It only intensifies the ache in my chest that Maxime should know my taste so well.

The overnight bag contains my toiletries and makeup. I shower, take my hair up like Maxime likes it, and apply a light coat of makeup before putting on the dress. It has a high neck and low back, the fabric kissing my breasts and legs. I haven't touched the new sewing machine yet. I wanted to focus on my sketches first. Now I'm not sure I can.

After fitting the strappy heels, I go out onto the balcony and let the breeze cool my skin as I inhale the fragrance of the night. Salt drifts in from the sea. It's mixed with the smell of industrial oil and grilled sausage wafting from the hotdog vendor on the street corner four stories below. It's the smell of night and the city, of potential and freedom. In Johannesburg, it was smoke and coal, fabric dye near the flea market, and leather coming from the shoe factory. Each city holds its own prison, a life I yearn to escape. Yet here I am, a prisoner of my own making, bound to the heart of a merciless man.

The door opens and closes. There's a silent pause. I imagine him crossing the floor on the soft carpet. A moment later, his heels fall hard on the balcony tiles.

He comes to a stop next to me. Citrus and cloves reach my nostrils, wiping the city and night away and its feeble promise of freedom.

"I have something for you." Taking my hand, Maxime turns me to face him. His gaze slips over me, evaluating my efforts. "You look beautiful."

We haven't laughed since the sewing machine. I was going to laugh with him tonight. I imagined us like this, at home, maybe on the beach, sharing a moment from my day. He'd pull me into his lap and make me tell him everything while listening attentively like he always does.

"You never tell me about your day," I say.

He drags his knuckles over my cheek. "You didn't drink the champagne I ordered for you."

"I've learned my own lesson."

He smiles. "One glass isn't going to hurt."

No, but it'll take the edge off, and I don't want to dull my senses tonight. I want to punish myself with the truth for being so repeatedly, stupidly naïve.

I don't know where the words come from. They're out before I can stop them. "You used me that night."

His look is amused. "The night you got drunk? You let me."

True.

Leaning closer, he brushes his lips over my neck. "You liked it."

I did.

"It's on the table," he says. "Go open your gift."

I don't want another one, but I don't have the energy to fight this war, too. I let him pull me back inside. A velvet box lies on the table. I flip the lid back to reveal a diamond choker. The stones are brilliant and beautifully set. It looks invaluable. It looks like a really expensive collar.

"Turn around," he says, lifting it from the velvet cushion.

I face the mirror, watching my reflection as he puts the choker around my neck and secures the clasp at the back. The woman who stares back at me isn't me. She's the woman who sold her body in exchange for a life and a reprieve from lessons, a woman who's just accepted another magnificent token of ownership.

Cupping my hips, he meets my eyes in the glass. "You're so perfect it hurts to look at you."

Yes, it hurts. I turn away from the picture, condemning it to the place where I lock away all my painful memories.

He takes my hand and kisses my fingers. "Every eye will be on you tonight."

When he puts my hand on his arm, I don't protest. I follow him out in the hallway and into the elevator. We exit on the first floor. The ballroom is already buzzing with people. I'm relieved it's a seated dinner and not a cocktail, which means I don't have to follow like a puppy while Maxime mingles. I can sit down and drift away while the speeches drone on.

A hostess shows us to our table. The hall fills up even more. Maxime pours me a glass of water. It seems the couple who were seated with us didn't show up, because when the speeches finally start, we're alone at our table.

Maxime drapes an arm around the back of my chair. He drags his fingers over my shoulder and along the curve of my neck to my nape where his thumb traces the choker before brushing over a vertebra.

Leaning over, he whispers in my ear, "Talk to me, Zoe."

I look at him. He wants to talk here? Now?

"You're upset," he says in a low voice. "Tell me. I'll make it right."

"You can't make it right," I whisper back.

"Try me."

Tears burn behind my eyes again. "I never entered that school on my own merit, did I?"

He stiffens. "Who told you?"

"No one. It wasn't that hard to figure out."

Anger sweeps over his features. "If you're being treated unfairly just because—"

"No." I don't want trouble for Madame Page. It's bad enough he forced my way in with his powerful family connections. "How did you do it? Did you donate a ridiculous amount of money to the school?"

His lips tighten. "No one says no to me, not in this city."

"I see." I look away so he won't see the tears I can't contain.

Gripping my chin, he turns my face back to him. "Is it so bad that I want to make you happy?"

"Yes, Maxime. This is bad. This is really bad."

"Why?" he asks though clenched teeth.

"You made me believe I *earned* it."

"You did," he says with conviction.

"That's not for you to decide. You're not a fashion design expert. It was up to the board and Madame Page."

He looks confused. "I thought you'd be happy."

"I *was* happy until I found out it's a lie."

Gripping my hand hard under the table, he says, "I pulled a lot of strings to make this happen for you, so you're going to swallow your pride and be a good girl and go to school and do what you love. It's that simple."

"You'd think it is."

"If you're implying I don't care, you're damn right. I don't give a damn what *Madame* or your classmates think. You shouldn't either."

I guess that's the difference between us, and the crux of the problem. He doesn't give a damn. Unfortunately, I do.

"No more talking about this," he says, bringing my hand to his lips and kissing my knuckles.

I breathe in deeply to abate my tears and put a stopper on my emotions. I can't give the people around us the satisfaction of witnessing my distress. It's too personal. Too vulnerable.

I eat as much as I can stomach, feeling raw inside. Feeling cheated. What else is Maxime hiding from me? I'm peeling away these layers of truth one at a time, and I'm scared of what I'll find at the core. I'm so tired of floating in the dark and drowning in his secrets.

It's after midnight when the dinner is finally over and Maxime has greeted everyone he wanted to. Networking is important.

"I know you're tired," he says, placing a palm on my lower back. "We can sleep here if you like."

"If you don't mind, I prefer to go home."

Home. It's not the first time I've said it tonight, but we both pause when the word leaves my lips. Maxime is kind enough not to make a big deal out of it, even as more of the possessive satisfaction I've come to recognize washes over his face. He tells Gautier to fetch my overnight bag from upstairs and ask at reception for a valet to bring his car around.

The same questions as always repeat through my mind when he escorts me outside. Why is Maxime keeping me here? I know it has something to do with the diamonds from the questions he posed before kidnapping me, but why is he holding Damian's life over my head? I'm distracted, but simultaneously hyperaware of the warm night and how the heat seems to lift for a brief reprieve even as Maxime's broad palm burns hot on the exposed skin of my back. Benoit and Gautier move ahead of us, Gautier carrying my overnight bag. The valet rounds the corner with Maxime's Bugatti. The Mercedes in which the guards came is parked across the street.

A black car with tinted windows rolls slowly down the road. The back window lowers when they're almost next to us. It must be someone Maxime knows, maybe someone from the party who wants to call out a last goodbye. I look at Maxime to catch his attention. He's slowed down beside me, staring at the car with a strange expression.

"Get down," Maxime yells at the same time as a string of shots blast through the air.

He throws his body in front of mine, taking me down to the pavement as the glass door of the casino explodes behind us. I hit the concrete with a thud, his arms cushioning the fall but my head taking a knock that makes my teeth clatter. My elbows and hip burn. My bones are crushed against the hard surface by Maxime's weight.

Another round of shots go off. People scream. The couple who exited behind us scurry for the casino lobby. My cheek is pressed to the pavement. The concrete is rough and warm against my skin. It smells of dust and car exhaust. I register everything as the black car speeds off.

Someone shot at us.

"Maxime!" I push on his shoulders. Oh, my God! Is he hurt?

His eyes are the color of pale marble, cold and hard, when he lifts his weight and drags his hands over my body in clinical, examining strokes. He's calm. Collected. Only his voice is urgent. "Are you hurt? Have you been shot, Zoe?"

"I'm fine."

"Fuck." He gets up and helps me to my feet.

Benoit is waving a gun. Gautier is lying in the gutter.

What? No! I slam a hand over my mouth.

Maxime bends down and presses two fingers on the jugular vein in Gautier's neck. His face hardens. "Follow them," he says to Benoit.

Benoit runs for the Mercedes.

"Get in the car, Zoe," Maxime says.

I'm aware of him touching my arm, dragging me a little, but I can't focus on anything other than the blood oozing from Gautier's temple. I can't look away from his open eyes and the way the light is missing from their depths.

"Zoe." Maxime's fingers dig into my upper arms. My teeth clack together as he shakes me. "I need you to keep it together. Can you do that for me, *cherie*?"

He turns me toward the Bugatti. The valet stands on the pavement with a stunned expression. I somehow manage to fold my stiff body double and get into the passenger seat when Maxime opens the door for me. He gets in and secures my safety belt, then his own.

Not looking back, he pulls off with screeching tires. We're driving too fast. It makes me nervous, especially with the narrow road and the steep abyss dropping into the sea. I grip the door handle as he dials Raphael on voice command.

"We have a situation at the casino," Maxime says when his father replies. "Gautier is down."

Raphael's voice is tight. "Motherfucking damn."

"I'm dealing with it. I'll keep you posted."

Maxime switches over to another call, telling someone he needs cleanup. Another call demands backup, the next puts the guards at the house on alert, and the last instructs his lawyer to take care of the police. By the time we arrive home, Maxime seems to have everything, including himself, under control.

It's only me who's shaking, unable to process what's happened.

He comes around and helps me from the car. The front garden is swarming with guards. Two stand at the door. Another waits inside.

"Guard her with your life," Maxime says.

"Yes, sir."

Maxime makes his way with long strides to the room he always keeps locked.

I run after him. "Maxime, wait!"

He takes a key from his pocket, unlocks the door, and pushes it open. Reflexively, I remain on the threshold when he hurries inside. It's an instinctive reaction to knowing he doesn't want me in there. There's a big desk against the window and photos on the walls. It looks like a study. He opens a tall safe in a corner cabinet and removes a gun that he pushes into his waistband.

"Maxime, please. What are—?"

The automatic rifle he takes out next makes my words dry up.

Without giving me another look, he locks the door and walks from the house.

I stand in the foyer, staring at the front door he slammed behind him, hearing the echo bouncing off the emptiness.

The guard catches my eyes. "Maybe you should have a drink," he says in a strong voice. "And a hot shower."

I rest a palm against the wall. My body is shaking with cold chills. The lie whispers past my lips. "I'm fine."

I want to be, but I'm not. Gautier is dead. Someone tried to kill Maxime in the middle of the street, right there in the open. That's not normal. That's not a simple drawback of being part of a rich and powerful family. That's not taking the law into your own hands to punish your brother. That's the truth. That's the little worm that's been niggling its way into my brain, the one I've been trying so hard to ignore.

Making my way to the stairs, I grip the balustrade. My back is straight for the sake of the guard who's still watching. He can't see my shaky knees as I make my way to Maxime's bedroom. I stop in front of the mirror. The beautiful dress is torn. My arms are scraped and dirty. My hair is a mess. My face doesn't look much better.

I function on autopilot. I strip, shower, disinfect the scrapes, and put ointment on the bruise on my hip where I hit the concrete. I dress in a T-shirt and soft cotton shorts, and go down to the kitchen to make a pot of tea. I carry it to the bedroom and install myself there, waiting for Maxime to return, telling myself it's my future I'm worried about and not his life.

CHAPTER 6

Maxime

Benoit followed the motherfuckers to a house near the hill. I park a distance away and gather my men around me. The backup arrived a few minutes before me.

"Whoever pulled the trigger," I say, "is mine."

They nod.

"How many?" I ask Benoit.

"Three guys got out of the car and entered the house. The curtains are pulled, but the light came on downstairs. The only other movement is on the first floor, second window to the left."

I cock my gun. "Let's go."

We creep along the shadows, staying low behind the bushes. The front door opens on the street. I motion for Benoit to go around the back. He returns promptly, giving me the all clear.

Gun pointed in front of me, I stand back for one of the men to kick down the door. I'm inside before the three motherfuckers on the couch can blink. Four of my men rush up the stairs.

"Put your hands on the table," I say, circling the three idiots.

The one on the left is the last to comply. He holds my eyes with defiance, his lip curled up in a mocking smile. It's him I choose. I've always loved a challenge.

"Tie these two up," I say to Benoit, motioning at the other two.

"With pleasure, sir," he replies with cold hatred just as my guards drag a man, dressed in black combat gear with his arms tied behind his back, down the stairs.

"Anyone else?" I ask.

"No, sir," one of my men says. "We've searched upstairs."

The other guards return from the kitchen. "No one else downstairs, sir."

Benoit binds the arms of the men on the couch. Except for the cocky one. Him, I push into a chair.

"Secure his feet and hands," I say.

My men work fast. They tie him to the chair and use more rope to bind his wrists to the armrests and his ankles to the legs of the chair.

"Who pulled the trigger?" I ask.

One of the fuckers glances at his friend tied up in the chair.

"I did." The guy in the chair spits at my feet.

I nod at Benoit. "Take the others to the warehouse. They're yours."

He gives me a look of appreciation. It's only fair that he gets to torture and kill them. Gautier was the closest thing he had to a brother.

Half of my men go with Benoit. The other half stay with me.

"You know how this works," I say, standing in front of the man who looks at me like I'm the one doing him the injustice. "Are you going to talk, or must I do my magic first?"

"Fuck you," he says with a grin.

I smile. Good. "I was hoping you'd say that." Taking my gun from my waistband, I aim at his hand.

One of my men shoves a dishcloth in his mouth. He clams his jaw shut on the fabric and clutches the armrest. I shoot off his trigger finger.

The silencer dampens the sound, but he screams like a baby behind the bundle of fabric.

"Who sent you?" I ask.

He's dragging in air through his nose, trying to breathe through the pain. The look he gives me when he can finally focus again says *fuck you*.

I shoot off his thumb. Flesh and splintered bone hang from the knuckle by shreds of skin.

He bleeds like a pig and cries like a pussy. I'd ice the stumps to stop him from bleeding out and shoot off every motherfucking finger and toe until he gives me the answers I want, but I don't have that much time. Zoe is home. Alone. I need to get back to her.

Pushing the gun on his left nut, I ask, "Who sent you?"

He mumbles behind the cloth. My man removes it.

He gulps in air, spit and gob mixing with his words. "*Brise de Mer.*"

This idiot isn't part of their family. He's a paid man. If this is about territory, why didn't they come after me themselves? I dig the barrel into his balls. "Why?"

"To take out the girl," he slobbers.

I go still. Every molecule in my body freezes in rage. I know exactly which girl. There's only one girl. There will only ever be one. Still, I grind out the question as atomic violence builds in my veins. "Which woman?"

He looks at me with pain-laced eyes. "*Your* woman. Zoe Hart."

The woman I've paraded for the world to see. The woman I've made a target by showing everyone how much she means to me. My cousin, Jerome, warned me the night I paid a million euros for her in the charity auction, but I was too dead set on showing everyone she belonged to me to care.

I move the barrel down his scrotum and wiggle it under his butt until it rests snugly over his asshole. "Why?"

"Because she's your weakness," he says on a rush, trying to lift his filthy ass away from the gun.

"You thought killing her would weaken me," I say with a cold laugh.

Sweat beads on his face. "Yes."

Fucking wrong. It would've crushed me. "Why are they targeting me?" They should've targeted my father if they wanted the organization to crumble.

"You're the backbone of the family."

I'm the brain. My father is a loose cannon, getting more unstable in his business decisions by the day. The only one who keeps him in line is me. They were hoping on avoiding a war and taking over by weakening the pillar that's keeping the house of cards from toppling.

Gripping his hair in my free hand, I pull back his head. "Who paid you?"

"Stefanu Mariani."

The Corsican underboss. I grin. "That wasn't so difficult now, was it?" I stare into the eyes of the man who was going to snuff out Zoe's life. "Tell me something, how did it feel to pull that trigger?"

He blinks. "What?"

"When you aimed at my woman, how did it feel?"

I relive the moment in stark fucking monstrous detail, the moment I realized they were going to shoot, the moment I felt nothing, not for me or my family or the business, but only for the woman at my side. The moment my heart beat only for her. The moment Gautier threw his body in front of us and took the bullets, three. One in the chest, one in the stomach, and one in the head.

"What's your name?" I ask.

"Dominic."

"What did you feel, Dominic?"

He frowns, incomprehension marring his ugly features. "Nothing."

Wrong fucking answer.

I pull the trigger.

CHAPTER 7

Maxime

On the way home, I call my father. What happened calls for retaliation. The Corsicans need to be shown who runs this city. No one puts a hit on my woman and lives to see daylight.

"You erred," my father says when I've filled him in. "Alexis had reason. We should've wiped out those Corsican bastards the minute they landed on our shore."

I hate to admit for once he's right. I gave them the benefit of the doubt because the Belshaws don't start wars. However, taking a hit at my woman is a fucking cowardice, honorless move, and it just started a genocide.

My fingers curl around the gearstick, my nails cutting into the leather. "I'm taking them all out."

"I'm calling in the Italians."

"I don't need the fucking Italians."

My father's voice rises. "We need them now more than ever. This is exactly why we secured the deal."

"I'll do my own cleanup in my backyard, thank you fucking very much."

"Son." My father sighs. "You can't pretend it's not happening forever."

I clench my jaw. "I'm not pretending."

"Is that why you're avoiding Leonardo?"

I shift gears so violently the gearbox screeches. "I'm not avoiding him. I'm just not in the mood for dragging a tail along."

"I know why you're doing it."

"Do *not* say her name to me. Not now." I'm too explosive.

Wisely, my father keeps his mouth shut.

"I'll let you know when it's done," I say before ending the call.

My father will summon more men and make sure their house is protected. He'll warn Alexis and do what he must. I dial our most effective muscle, one of the men I sent to torture the other motherfucker mercenaries. By now he should have the information I want.

"Where are the Corsicans?" I ask when he answers.

"Meeting as we speak."

Probably weaponing up, knowing their murder attempt failed and we're coming after them.

"They're gathered in a warehouse in the industrial area."

"Blow it up."

"Yes, sir."

By sunrise, no *Brise de Mer* will be left in our territory. Our message will have been delivered. Crystal fucking clear.

My first stop is at Gautier's mother's house. She's a widow, living alone. Fuck. He was her only child, but he knew the risks. He took the bullets knowing she'd want for nothing. We take care of our own, especially of the relatives of those who sacrifice their lives.

I ring the bell.

Her face crumples when she opens the door and sees my face. She knows what this visit means.

"I'm sorry." I grip her shoulder. "He died bravely."

"How?" she asks, her wrinkled eyes dry but sorrow drifting in their depths.

"Drive-by shooting. The men who did this paid. They died slowly."

Her body wilts under my hold, her shoulders folding inward and her spine curling.

I squeeze gently. "Do you have someone to call? Someone who can be with you?"

She nods.

I hand her my card. "You call me. For anything. Any time. Night or day."

She shuts the door.

I leave her to her grieving. There's not much else I can do. Nothing to make it better. Not even time erases this pain.

I get back into the car and make sure I'm not tailed. Driving like a maniac, I head toward Cassis. I only realize how cold I am when I park at the house. I'm eager to go inside, to see Zoe, but I check in with the guards and schedule a shift to make sure everyone remains vigilant before checking the perimeter alarms. Only then do I allow myself to enter and face the fact that I could've lost her tonight. That I most certainly—gladly—would've taken the bullets meant for her if Gautier hadn't.

I shut the door softly. If she's sleeping, I don't want to wake her. I shrug out of my jacket and dump it on the chair in the entrance. I'm halfway across the foyer when she comes down the stairs. Stopping in my tracks, I drink her in as she approaches. She's showered and clean, dressed in a loose T-shirt and a pair of shorts, and I'm pathetically grateful. I don't know how wild my emotions would've run if I'd seen her in her tattered dress and dirt-streaked face.

"You all right?" I ask when she stops in front of me. My vocal cords are tight. They feel unused.

She places her hands on my chest. "You?"

I cup her palms, let her warmth sink into my cold skin. "Yes."

"What happened?" she whispers.

I want to kiss her. I want to fuck her. I want to just hold her.

Instead, I let her go. If I touch her in any way, I'll go overboard. I may say things, things I can't mean. Instead, I walk to the library and sink down in the chair behind the desk.

She follows quietly, her bare feet not making a sound on the Turkish carpets. At the liquor tray, she pours a whiskey the way I like and carries the glass to me. Our fingers brush when I take it.

"Thank you," I say, my words laced with surprise at the act of kindness when I deserve nothing of the kind.

She stands in front of the desk, her pretty face so pale I can count every freckle on her nose. "Is he...?" She swallows. "Gautier. Is he—?"

"Dead."

She flinches. Tears blur the blue of her eyes. "I'm so sorry, Maxime."

I take a swallow of the drink. The burn is good. It loosens up my voice, making it easier to speak. "So am I, but not as much as his poor mother."

"Where were you?"

"You shouldn't have waited up. It's late."

"You think I can sleep?"

I hand her the glass.

She turns it and places her lips on the exact spot where the glass touched mine before drinking, then puts it back in my hand. It's become our game. "Were you at the police station, giving a statement?"

I look at her. She says it flatly, her back straight. She doesn't believe it. I bet her question is just one of a long list she's rehearsed to flush out the truth.

"No," I say.

"I heard what you told Benoit about following that car. Did you go after him, the man who killed Gautier?"

"Yes."

Her chest rises with a breath. Her posture is brave, but her hands are shaking. She can't hide the turmoil in her eyes. "Did you kill him?"

I look straight into those pretty baby blues. "Them. I killed *them*."

If at all possible, she goes even whiter. "What are you, Maxime?"

My smile is wry. "A man."

I've never been more of a man since the day I met her. She made me a man who reacts to a woman in the most primal of ways. She made me a man with a weakness, a man with chest full of fear. Most of all, I'm just a man of flesh and blood, a man who wants to live to protect the person he cares about the most in the world.

Zoe plants her palms on the desk, facing me with all forty-six kilos of her feistiness. Her words are measured, each one articulated. "What are you, Maxime? Mafia?" She spits out the word like it's poison.

"You know what I am."

She slams a palm down in front of me. "Say it."

Her anger only makes me smile broader. It's the irony of being caught in a trap I designed for her. It's the knowledge that this little flower has slain me. "Yes, I'm mafia, but you knew that all along."

Fire dances along the tears in her brilliant eyes. "I did *not*."

This changes anything? She thinks I'll let her go? Pretending to be ignorant makes fucking me easier for her?

"Oh, come on, Zoe. Not even you can be that naïve."

She jerks as if I've slapped her. Fine. It was a low blow. Her naivety is part of what I love about her. She's the light to my hell, the hope to my infernal darkness. Men like me are born dark. We're born into the darkness. We inherit it from our fathers and pass it on to our sons. She's the only brightness I'll ever have in my life, and I don't want her as anything other than herself, but she's changing regardless. It happens right in front of my eyes as her features contort with pain. She tries hard to bury her feelings under a mask of indifference, but that's *my* specialty. She's an open book, a flower for the plucking.

"Fuck you, Maxime." Her chin trembles, but she straightens and pulls her shoulders square. "You're right. I'm too naïve. Maybe I was hiding my head in the sand when you took me from my home to teach me your sick lessons, but it was the only way I could cope with what was happening to me, so fuck you again for your petty insults."

"Says the woman who just insulted me twice."

Her dainty nostrils flare. "You could've died tonight, and I don't know why I even care."

I lift a brow. "Is there a point to this conversation?"

She regards me for the longest moment. Her voice is soft but complex, wrapped in layers of weariness, fear, and desperation when she finally speaks. "I want to go home."

"No, you don't."

Her voice rises in anger. "You don't know what I want."

"I know you better than you think."

She balls her small hands into fists at her sides. "I want to go home."

"This is your home, Zoe. You've admitted it yourself, more than once. There's nothing left for you in Johannesburg. This is your dream. This is the life you've always wanted. You want to run because you know who I am now. You want to run because of what you've lived through tonight. It's only natural, but I'm here to protect you. I'll always protect you." Even from my grave.

She's shivering like a daisy in a storm, but she's standing her ground. "If they took a shot at you, you must be important."

If they took a shot at you. Her words still me. She notices. Fuck. It's a heavy truth to lay on her shoulders, but I can't protect her if I keep her head pushed down in the sand.

"How important, Maxime? If you won't let me go, it's only fair that I know."

She's right. I wanted to keep her away from the business, but ignorance gets you killed. Especially now that she'll be attending school in town. Especially now that she'll have triple the guards protecting her day and night. I made an error in showing the world how much she means to me, but I won't let her pay the price.

"Quite important," I say.

"You're not the boss or something like that?" she asks with a nervous laugh.

"Not yet. I still share the power with my father."

Placing a hand over her stomach, she looks at me as if she sees the monster in my soul. "Oh, my God."

"We'll put extra security measures in place. You'll take double the number of guards with you to school."

"Me?" She gives me a wide-eyed look. "It's not me they were after. What if they kill you?"

That coldness spreads through me again. I bury it under the fury and violence still coursing through my veins, but Zoe is perceptive. I may have made it my job to get to know her, but she's gotten to know me in the process, too.

"Unless," she says with a soft gasp, "they weren't after you."

"Zoe." I get to my feet, but she takes a step away.

"They came after me," she says with those big, haunted eyes. I can almost see the gears turning in her head. I see the exact moment she connects the dots. "To get to you."

I stand helplessly, my hands hanging loosely at my sides while the truth turns her face into a mask of horror. I can't tell her it won't happen again. I can't tell her I'll let her go. I can only round the desk and offer her my arms.

"No." She holds up a hand and takes two more steps away from me. "Don't touch me."

Her words hit me like no bullet can. "I'm not going to let anything happen to you."

"You can't promise that," she says on a panicked whisper. "What happens if you're killed?"

I opt for the truth. It's better to give her these weapons than to make her vulnerable by not enlightening her. "It's an option we shouldn't exclude, but I'll make sure you're looked after."

Her breath catches. "That's not what I meant. What happens to me, stuck here in this city without a passport?"

I approach cautiously, like with an injured animal. "You don't have to worry about that. It's my job to take care of the details."

"It's my life. *My* fucking life."

"Zoe." My patience is running thin. It's been a long night. "Don't start."

She folds her arms around her stomach. "A man died because of me."

I slowly continue my advance. "He knew what the job entailed when he signed up."

"Is Damian involved in the mafia? Is that why you're keeping me?"

Stopping, I rub a hand over my face.

"Damn you, Maxime. Tell me! *A man died tonight.*"

The implied meaning hangs in the air. It could've been her. Tilting my head toward the ceiling, I sigh. "Damian is involved with his own mafia in prison. It's got nothing to do with us."

"Then why keep me?"

I wasn't going to tell her, but the game is no longer the same. I'm never letting her go. What difference does it make if she knows? She's right. After tonight, it only seems fair.

Taking a deep breath, I say, "Your brother is planning on taking back a diamond deposit he discovered. The mine currently belongs to Harold Dalton."

"Dalton?" she exclaims. "The man who put Damian in prison?"

"Yes. He stole Damian's discovery and framed him."

"What does that have to do with you?"

"Dalton sells the diamonds directly to us, cutting out the middleman. We want to make sure your brother will sell to us when he takes over."

She gapes at me. "You're that certain Damian will succeed?"

"I've been privy to his plans. My money is on him."

"Just in case, you needed something to blackmail Damian."

My look is level. "Yes."

"That's why you took me." The revelation settles slowly in her eyes. "You were never going to hurt Damian. You need him." Her lips part on a soundless gasp. "You lied to me."

I don't deny it.

Anger washes over her features. "You twisted the truth. You used me. You made me submit to you with a lie. I could've defied you," she says with disbelief. "I could've run. Nothing would've happened to my brother."

I close the distance between us. "One way or another, I had to bring you here. I chose the non-violent way."

Her entire body trembles as the betrayal peels away. Finally, she sees what she's fallen for—the real me, the monster hidden beneath a well-cut suit bearing gifts and kindness. She sees through my plan, and she knows it's too late. She's already caught in my web.

"Why are you telling me now?" she asks, shaking so much her jaw quakes. "You're never going to let me see my brother again, are you? That's why you don't care that I know. I can't tell Damian the truth if I never see him again."

Cupping her cheek, I stroke a thumb over that trembling jaw. "I won't let you go, Zoe. Not in four years. Never. You're mine. Your place is here." I apply the gentlest of pressure, making her pretty lips pout. "What you better understand is it won't end well for you if you run. I will always find you."

She grips my forearms as her knees buckle under the weight of the truth. It's a sugar-coated threat, but she's learned enough lessons to let her imagination run wild with consequences.

I give her time to process it. I give her space when she shoves me away. Her fingers flitter to her lips as she looks around the room like a trapped animal.

"Too much has happened tonight," I say. "Let me take care of you."

"How?" she asks with a mocking laugh. "By locking me up? By lying to me?"

"By taking you to bed. The sun will be up soon. You need to rest."

"If Damian finds out I'm here, what will you tell him?"

"That you're here because you want to be."

She looks at me as if I've slapped her. "How will you explain a lie like that?"

"I went to South Africa to meet with Dalton about business. We had dinner and shared a bottle of wine. I asked about the diamond discovery. He told me about Damian, and how your brother stole a diamond from his house and ended up in prison. I found that hard to believe, seeing that Damian discovered a riverbed full of them. My curiosity was piqued, so I looked you up. One thing led to another."

"Just like that," she says, the strange look on her face not wavering.

"Yes. Now come to bed."

Turning her back on me, she walks to the liquor tray. A drink is probably a good idea. A little alcohol will help her sleep. A glass falls over. She's anything but steady. I cross the floor to help her, and then stop dead as she spins around, pushing the icepick against my chest.

CHAPTER 8

Zoe

The compassion in Maxime's eyes only makes me want to kill him more. This man has betrayed me in so many ways. He lied about killing Damian. He stole me. He stole my virginity. He kept the fact that he's a mafia boss conveniently hidden from me. He teaches me cruel lessons. He controls every aspect of my life. By claiming me, he's put me in danger. He knew how his secrets would impact me, yet he made me dependent on him. He trapped me with his sick games, physically and emotionally, and now I'll always be a pawn for his opponents to get to him. This is as much as I can take.

I push the sharp point of the icepick a little harder, letting it pierce the fabric of his shirt. "Give me the passport you used to smuggle me out of South Africa."

His lips lift in one corner. "When you have it, what are you going to do with it?"

"I'm going to leave," I say through clenched teeth. "You're going to give me money and a car, and you're going to let me go."

He raises an eyebrow. "Go where?"

"Where you'll never find me."

"A place like that doesn't exist, little flower. I'll turn the world upside down if I have to, and you'll only end up right back here."

It makes me feel like a hamster running in place in a wheel. So futile. "Give it to me!" I push harder, feeling the barrier of his strong chest against the weapon.

He looks down at me, his arms resting at his sides. "Go ahead. Stab me, Zoe. You'll want to move the tip up a centimeter and a fraction to the left if you want to hit my heart."

I do it. I follow his guidance and let the point rest against his heart. He's killing me little by little, destroying what's left of me. I can't live like this anymore.

His cold, gray eyes mock me. "What are you waiting for?"

I put my weight behind the pick. I'm shaking so much it's hard to keep the shaft steady. The point meets more resistance, hard muscle and scarred flesh. How many kisses have I planted on that flesh? How many times have I traced his imperfect skin to hear him exhale with a shudder? How many nights have I harbored hope in my chest, hope to escape, hope that he'll return a drop of my feelings? Because if he doesn't, I'm afraid I'll lose my soul. My unrequited affection will slowly poison me. The bitterness of being forever unloved and eternally lonely will chip away at my heart until nothing but hard, polished hate is left. I hate him as much as I love him, but I hate myself more for loving him. It's the worst suffering. Insupportable.

Tears pool in my eyes as I try to harm him. I have to do this. I have to save myself. I start crying when he doesn't stop me as I push harder. A crimson drop flowers over the fabric of his shirt. It's the color of life, of love. It's the color of him. Beneath it all, he's exactly what he said—just a man.

My fingers loosen around the shaft. Every bone in my body shakes. The icepick falls with a clatter on the floor. It's a harsh sound, cruel and devastating. A sob tears from my chest.

Moving like lightning, he grabs my wrist. Even if my hand is empty now, his hold is like an iron shackle. The other hand finds purchase in my hair. He yanks my head back with force and crushes our mouths together. The kiss is as brutal as the threat I couldn't carry out. He forces me onto my knees by my hair, following me down to the floor.

The sting on my scalp makes my eyes water as he unbuckles his belt and unzips his fly. Stretching out over me, he pushes my shorts and underwear over my hips and grabs the root of his cock in his hand. I barely have time to take a breath before he impales me, thrusting so deep it hurts. I cry out, tears of defeat leaking from the corners of my eyes.

Is this what I've reduced myself to? A killer? I don't want to become like him. More so, I can never harm him. It's twisted, but I can control it as little as I can control my love. I care way too much.

Placing a palm over the bloodstain on his shirt, I whisper, "I'm sorry."

He lifts up on one arm and scans my face with his solemn, gray gaze. "I know."

He spears his fingers through my hair, caressing my scalp and wiping away the hurt. Framing my face between his palms, he kisses my eyes and cheeks. He kisses my lips as he starts moving, setting a slow pace. I rock in his arms, letting his gentle strength soothe me. I fall deeper under his spell as his body calls and mine answers. I bow to his magic, gasping into his mouth as my back arches from the pleasure. It's different than how we normally fuck. It's desperate, yet tender. It's a celebration of life. I could've lost him tonight. My threat of killing him was all bluffing, nothing but manipulation to let me go. I don't want him dead. Yet his life is dangerous. I can lose him every day. To live this fear over and over, day after day, I'm not sure I can do it.

I gasp into our kiss. "I'm scared."

He wipes the tears from my cheeks with his thumbs. "You're brave."

"Not enough."

"You underestimate yourself."

I moan when he hits a barrier deep inside. The trauma of tonight makes everything that's churning in my chest spills out. "Will you love me?"

He smiles. For once, the gesture isn't mocking or haughty, but kind. "Am I not loving you now?"

"You know what I mean." I need more than making love. I need the love that bleeds red, the kind that flows from his heart.

A trace of regret softens his features. "I've given you all I'm capable of."

At least this is the one thing he's honest about. Maxime will never be able to love me. The pain is dazzling. It's pure. It's beautiful, because it's born from love. It only hurts as deep as you feel.

Pressing his lips on my ear, he offers me a consolation. He dangles temptation. "Let me give you what I have."

I'm not strong enough. I give in. I follow his lead, rolling my hips to his tempo when he pushes a hand between our bodies to find my clit. I snake my arms around his neck, holding him close to me. I take his pleasure, and give him mine. As I come around him, he comes inside, filling me with his essence for the first time, giving me all that he has.

I'm boneless in the aftermath, depleted by the emotional turmoil and extreme pleasure. Maxime adjusts our clothes, gathers me in his arms, and carries me upstairs. We shower together. When I try to wash away the blood from the nick I've left on his skin, he brushes my hand away. The old Maxime is back, unsettlingly intense and slightly distant.

In bed, he pulls me against his body.

Leaning my head on his shoulder, I trace the bumpy skin of his torso. "Why haven't you come inside me before?"

He stares at the ceiling, gently brushing a palm over my arm, and says in his beautiful accent, "I didn't want to ruin you."

"Ruin me?" I frown. "Ruin me how?"

His voice is like a far-off star in the dark—elusive and intangible, untouchable like every other part of him. "You're pure."

"And now?" I stroke a hand down his stomach to trace the line of hair that starts under his navel. His choice of words makes me smile. "Am I impure?"

His tone is solemn. "Now you're mine."

I trail my palm farther south, cupping his erection. "I thought you said I was that already."

"This is different."

I squeeze gently. "How?"

"Now," he says, still not meeting my eyes, "you're my property."

I still. The declaration slices through me. I didn't think it was possible for him to hurt me more. I pull away from him with a wry smile. I guess that's Maxime, honest to the point of cutting me to the bone.

"Thanks for telling me," I say. "I thought it might've been something a little less coldhearted like enjoying the intimacy of such an act with your fuck toy."

He removes his arm from around me and sits up. Soft light washes over the room when he flicks on the nightstand lamp. Flashing me with a view of his hard, naked body, he walks to the dressing room and closes the door. A short moment later, he exits dressed in sweatpants and a T-shirt, carrying a sports bag.

My gaze is drawn to the bag. "What are you doing?"

He drops the bag on the floor and sits down next to me. "Spread your arms and legs."

My breath catches. "What?"

His look is gentle, encouraging even. "You heard me."

"Why?"

"I'm going to tie you up."

My mouth goes dry. "Why?"

"Spread them, Zoe. I don't want to use force with you after what happened tonight."

Fear snakes up my spine. "Are you going to hurt me?"

"I'll never hurt you." His smile doesn't reach his eyes. "I may frustrate you."

"You're into kink?" I ask, even if it shouldn't surprise me. He's virile, and he has a strong libido. He's also depraved and lacks a moral compass. I bet he's into worse than kink. "You're not into torture, are you?"

His eyes tighten. "I'm not my brother."

Wrong thing to say. His brother seems to be a trigger for his anger. Impatiently, he grips my wrist and lifts it above my head. I keep still because I don't have a choice. I can't fight him off. Doing so will only stimulate his excitement. Maxime loves it when I fight.

My pulse jumps when he takes four coils of rope from the bag. Everything inside me wants to resist, but I'm powerless as he binds me spread-eagled to the bed. It's what he takes out of the bag next that makes me regret my surrender.

"What the hell is that?" I ask, staring at the purple vibrator mounted on a rubber sling and a silicone plug with a flat stopper.

"Sex toys."

"I'm not in the mood, Maxime."

He gives me an apologetic smile. "I know."

He takes a tube of lube from the bag and applies a copious amount to the butt plug and vibrator before inserting both gently. He wiggles the vibrator until the bulbous end fits snugly inside and the smaller one on my clit, then pulls the sling over my folds at the front and through my ass cheeks at the back to attach it to a belt he straps around my waist. Like this, the toys can't slip free.

"Do I need to gag you?" he asks.

"No," I cry out. "I don't like to feel that helpless."

He drags a finger from my temple to my jaw. "Then not a sound, understand?" Taking a small remote from the bag, he pushes on a button. The vibrator starts humming softly. He kicks it up two notches until the vibration penetrates my G-spot and clit. It's pleasant, but not so intense that I want to come.

"Comfortable?" he asks in a husky voice.

I give a nervous nod.

Gripping the sheet, he covers my body. "The toy has eight hours of battery life. After last night, we weren't going anywhere today, anyway."

Wait. What? He can't mean what I'm thinking.

He bends down and kisses my forehead. His deep voice is pure evil. "Sleep well, my little flower."

"You can't leave me like this."

He turns for the door.

"Wait," I call when he grips the handle. "Untie me, Maxime. Please."

He doesn't answer.

"Why are you doing this?" I cry out.

He turns back to face me. "Tonight was the first and last time you threatened my life. I gave you one chance only. You wasted it. It'll never happen again." He drags his gaze one more time over my sheet-covered body before stepping out and closing the door.

I can't believe it. He's serious. He's punishing me by leaving me like this until the vibrator battery runs flat. Indignant anger heats my veins as other parts of my body heat with unwanted arousal. I try to mentally override the sensations by focusing on my vexation, but the physical won't be denied. I feel because I'm human. I become needy despite my desire not to.

The setting is too low to get me off quickly. It takes a long time, and finally I'm so frustrated I wiggle and squirm to set the orgasm off. The relief is instantaneous and intense, but brief. My clit is oversensitive. I can barely tolerate the uninterrupted hum penetrating my flesh and bones. Moving in an attempt to escape the torturous stimulation doesn't help. The toy is strapped on too tightly.

After suffering the relentless vibrations for the longest time ever, pleasure starts to build anew. My need climbs. I'm wet, and it only makes it worse. Somehow, the assault on my lower body parts feels more intense, or maybe it's just because my body is so sensitive after the first orgasm. The need for release rises slowly, driving me to tears. It's like a rubber band that stretches and stretches. When the tension finally breaks, I'm panting. Unfortunately, this time I hardly feel the release, because the need is as constant now as the unbearable sensitivity of my flesh. My clit throbs, and my folds are swollen. My nipples remain hard. My lower body contracts as another cycle of need commences.

I'm clenching my teeth not to make a sound. I won't give Maxime the satisfaction. By the time the sun is bright and high, I'm drenched in sweat, and the sheet around my sex is soaked. It hurts to come, but I can't stop. Every cycle is agonizingly slow, the constant need always outweighing the brief release. It becomes so intense my whole body pulls tight with spasms until my toes curl. My muscles ache. There's a strange burning sensation on the soles of my feet. My hair sticks to my forehead. When another cruel climax takes over my body, my eyes roll back in my head.

At some point during the afternoon, I'm so exhausted I fall asleep, only to be woken with another release that tears me apart. I don't know how many times I come, only that when the battery finally hums too weak to wrench more agony from my body, I sink into the mattress with a sob of relief. It's like falling into a weightless void. It's only when I'm able relax my muscles for the first time that I realize how tense they've been drawn all day. I'm aching all over, but at last I can escape into the blissful reprieve of darkness.

CHAPTER 9

Maxime

The thought of Zoe coming around a vibrator in my bed is a temptation impossible to resist. I go to my study and lock the door behind me before activating the security camera, letting the image reroute to my laptop. I enable sound, too. I told her not to make noise. I can't let her get away with anything, not after she pushed an icepick against my heart and broke my skin. Not after the attempt on her life last night. Her obedience is all the more important. As long as she obeys me, I can keep her safe. It's defiance that opens opportunities for my opponents and puts her at risk.

With her dark hair spread over my pillow and her naked limbs stretched under the sheet, she's too beautiful to be human. I wish I'd left her uncovered to better appreciate the view, but her body temperature will eventually drop from exhaustion, and I didn't want her to be cold.

Watching her wrestle with her arousal, I take the tupper dish Francine had given me yesterday from the windowsill and place it in front of the laptop on my desk. I flick the lid off with a finger. The inhabitant immediately raises its tail. It's a *buthus occitanus*, a black scorpion. Francine found it in the kitchen. They're hardy little buggers to kill, so she threw a plastic container over the invader and slid the lid underneath to catch it inside. It tries to climb out of its prison, but the container is too deep.

A moan pulls my gaze to the screen. Head thrown back, Zoe orgasms so hard I can see her body convulse under the sheet. I smile. She's gorgeous when she comes. I'm looking forward to witnessing every one of her climaxes. I wonder how many times she'll come.

The scorpion turns inside the container. Leaning forward, I study it. Their venom isn't deadly. There are plenty of the small species around here. They favor the rocky landscape. Every year, we find at least a dozen in the garden.

I'm not a huge cigar fan like my father, but I light one now and suck on the end until the tip glows red. I'm a punishment behind, tonight excluded. I never made up for the night I fucked Zoe like a whore in the hotel.

Taking a big drag on the cigar, I roll the smoke around in my mouth before exhaling it into the container. It makes the scorpion furious. They don't like smoke. It swings its claws in the air, snapping its pinches together. I inhale and blow on it again, aggravating the little creature. Smoke is a danger. Its instinctive reaction is to escape that danger and to protect itself by attacking whatever threatens its life. When it's in full-blown survival mode, I stick my finger in the container.

It behaves exactly like it should. It hollows its back and zaps me with the sharp tip of its tail.

Motherfucking Jesus.

It hurts like a bitch. The burn is like nothing I've felt before. It creeps through my finger and up my arm, setting fire to my veins. It's different to the flames that cooked my skin. That burn came from the outside and melted inward with pain. This one starts on the inside, burning outward until it feels like my nails may peel back from my skin.

"Good job, buddy," I say as I sink back into my chair with grunts of agony.

I don't cut off my blood circulation to prevent the poison from spreading. I eat it up eagerly, letting my body's natural functioning carry it farther. My heart pumps faster. My blood flows stronger. The poison burns in my shoulder and down my chest. Sweat breaks out over my body.

Zoe comes.

Perfect. Beautiful.

I take a last drag of the cigar before putting the tip out on my finger, right on the sting.

Fuck, that hurts.

It sizzles and burns, killing one pain with another, but the affected parts of my body continue to hum as the venom works through my system, and Zoe starts crying from frustration.

The only way I can handle her tears is if I hurt myself worse than I'm hurting her. This isn't hurt for Zoe per se—I didn't lie about not physically hurting her—but sexual suffering can sometimes be worse. Her agony is riveting. It stokes my fire, making a different kind of poison burn in my blood. I want her lips around me. I want to fuck her mouth and come down her throat while agony rips through me, while three kinds of fire are wracking my body.

I unzip and take my cock in my hand. I'm so hard I'm aching. Going to my flower now won't serve tonight's lesson. She's got to live this one out alone. I stroke a couple of times, making the burn in my arm brighter. Closing my fist, I squeeze hard and rip my hand up and down. I let the cocktail of pain fuel me, mixing rough pleasure with agonizing suffering and twisted stalking on a laptop screen until my balls draw up and violent release erupts.

I catch my seed in my injured hand. It irritates the cigar burn. Using the en-suite toilet, I clean up. I'm still hurting. It's difficult to breathe. The poison must've spread to my chest. It'll fizzle out there, the crippling effect slowly diminishing. By the time eight hours are over, my pain will be gone.

Taking the container, I unlock the patio door and go out into the garden. A good distance away from the house and the path to the beach, I tip the container over. The scorpion scurries for freedom. It covers a good distance before hiding under a rock. I straighten and let my gaze linger on the house, on the window of the room where my flower is a prisoner spread in a spider's web made of ropes and lust. There's no more freedom for her now. There's no escaping my poison.

CHAPTER 10

Zoe

I wake up to the smell of rose petals. Blinking, I sit up. My hands and feet are untied. The toys are gone. The sheet lies discarded at my feet. Maxime sits on the edge of the bed, still dressed in the sweatpants and T-shirt from earlier.

He hands me a porcelain cup. "I brought you an infusion."

I reach for the offering with mixed feelings. I'm thirsty and the tea smells delicious, but I don't want to take anything from him, not after what he did. My body aches everywhere. Fighting an internal battle, I contemplate if I'm going to accept his peace offering. In the end, my dry throat wins. I take the cup from him and fold my palms around it.

"It's not too hot," he says. "I reckoned you'd be thirsty."

Damn right. I give him a cutting look as I sip the brew. It's become my favorite since he made me try it in Venice. It's not only the herbal tea that makes the room smell of flowers. The scent is stronger than just the rose petal tea. My gaze falls on a small ornate glass container on the nightstand filled with golden liquid.

"Drink up," he says, "and then lie down."

I tense. "Why?"

"I need to take care of you."

My tone is scathing. "Does your care involve ropes?"

He chuckles. "Only rose oil."

I look at the bottle. "It smells good."

"It's pure. I had it brought in from Grasse this morning. It took forty-thousand roses to fill that little bottle, and I'm going to drench your body in it."

I feel like slapping him. The only thing preventing me is the promise I made to myself and him not to ever do it again. "I'm angry with you."

His lips quirk. "I'm sure you are. However, I bet you've learned your lesson."

"Multiple orgasms? Who knew it could be such an effective method of torture?"

"I'll take that as an affirmative."

When he reaches for the cup, I gulp down the last of the tea. "What's with this thing you have for roses, anyway?"

"You," he says, taking the cup from my hand and leaving it on the nightstand.

"Me?"

"You always smell of roses."

"I do?" I blink. "You noticed?"

"There's not anything about you I don't notice. Now lie down."

Cautiously, I shift down the mattress. I'm still not sure I trust him not to inflict some other kind of punishment.

"Your lesson is over," he says as if reading my mind.

I relax a little. I still have much to process after last night. I'm drowning in guilt when I think of Gautier's mother. I'll never trample on the enormous gift of his life by being ungrateful, but a small part of me wishes he hadn't left me with this guilt. Maybe it would've been easier if he'd let me take the bullets meant for me. Shame burns in my stomach for the thought. I'm alive thanks to him. The least I can do is honor him by living it as well as I can. I just have to figure out how to cope with the truth Maxime finally shared with me last night. The deceit is a bitter pill to swallow. I thought I couldn't forgive him for cheating and lying about my admission into a top fashion design school, but this is so much worse. This betrayal goes even deeper. I hate him. I hate him with every fiber of my being. I hate that I care about him, and I hate that I need him even more. I hate what he's doing to me, and I'm powerless to prevent it.

The very subject of my turbulent thoughts rubs his knuckles over my breast.

"Turn over."

I don't want to react, but I can't stop it. The tip contracts. More shame churns in my stomach until acid pushes up in my throat.

"Turn over, Zoe," he says in that sinful accent, his tone non-negotiable.

I turn onto my stomach. At least I can hide my face and his effect on me. A few cold drops dribble on my back. I suck in a breath. When he starts rubbing the oil into my skin with his big, warm hands, I almost forget to think. He finds every knot in my shoulders, every tense spot that aches because of last night's strain, and takes his time to massage the hurt away. He moves down my back to my glutes, legs, and feet, and then my arms before finally massaging my scalp. I can't help but succumb to how good it feels. Like everything Maxime does, he's an expert at this, too. I'm all but melting into the mattress by the time he's done, my body buzzing drunkenly on relaxation. I've only slept for a couple of hours, so I'm about to doze off when he clicks his tongue in disapproval and says, "I'm not done yet."

The mattress dips as he lifts. I tense a little again, some of the agreeable fuzziness evaporating. Turning my head to the side, I watch him. He's pulling the T-shirt over his head, exposing his powerful, scarred chest and broad shoulders. Holding my eyes, he pushes the tracksuit pants over his hips. I trace the deep line of the V that cuts to his groin and the semi-hard cock that hangs heavy between his legs.

After the night I had, I don't want to have sex, but my conditioned body turns wet looking at him. His body is like a statue chiseled from stone. Every muscle is perfectly cut. His cock grows hard under my stare, making my mouth water. The warm, velvety flesh isn't the same as a plastic toy. Not at all. If he can't give me affection, he can give me pain and lust to forget just for a moment how much I hate both of us. I'm already his whore. What's one time more? Nothing in the scheme of bigger things. I can't go back to the virgin I was when he found me. I can't undo the sinful things we've done. Does it really matter if I'm knee-deep or sinking?

Maxime climbs back onto the bed. Dragging his palms up my legs, he spreads them and kneels between my thighs. My body jumps to life. My over-stimulated and over-used parts swell and turn slick. I can stop my reaction as little as I can turn off my love. He's trained me too well. He's a mastermind. The way he played and caught me in his game is brilliant, really.

Stretching out over me, he brushes my hair over one shoulder and kisses the shell of my ear. "I assume your pussy has had enough."

I can never have enough of him. It makes me want to break down with sobs. All I can do is close my eyes and bite my lip in futile denial.

"Get up on your knees for me, *cherie*." He assists me with a hand around my waist. "Lean down on your forearms. It'll better support your weight."

When he's arranged me the way he wants me, my legs are wide open and my ass in the air. I'm stretched open and on show. A flush of heat spreads over my cheeks as I look back and see where his gaze is trained.

His eyes darken. The frosty gray turns into that molten mercury I've come to associate with his lust. Taking his cock in his hand, he grabs the bottle of oil from the nightstand, tips it over his shaft, and stroke a few times to lubricate it. He drags his palm up and down and rolls it over the thick head of his cock. The wet sounds he makes with his hand as he all but masturbates right in front of my eyes turn me on more. I'm still processing this new discovery, storing it away with the rest of my shameful ones when he dribbles the oil in the crease between my globes and uses the slick head of his cock to spread the oil around my dark entrance.

I grip a fistful of sheet in each hand when he leans forward, applying pressure on the tight ring of muscle.

His voice is strained, his accent sounding stronger. "Do you want this, Zoe?"

Zis for *this*. Rounded like a full-bodied wine. The pronunciation drips sensuality. If I get drunk on it, I won't hear the lies.

"Use your voice," he says.

I let go, surrendering my grip to the quicksand of my body's betrayal. "Yes."

Easing forward slightly, he teases me. "Why?"

"Because it feels wrong."

"You're such a good little bad girl," he says, leaning over to caress my breasts and play with my nipples while sliding his cock deeper.

It doesn't hurt like before. I've been stretched all night, ready to take him.

"I need to fuck you hard," he whispers through clenched teeth, "after last night."

Last night.

Neither of us can get it out of our heads. It's a tipping point in time. Our dynamic has shifted. He used to hold back with me, never coming inside my body. I was the fool who silently begged him to let go. I asked for it. I wanted his everything. He reciprocated by giving it. Now that he's marked me, I'm his property, something he can no longer let go. Not after four years. Not ever.

Fuck, I'm such an idiot. I took the noose from his hands and put it around my neck myself. All because he made me love. He made me need more, but he's empty now. He's given everything he was capable of giving. There's no love in his heart, and there will never be. If my heart's to survive, I'll have to find my happiness elsewhere. Even if I got in by cheating, I'll pour my soul into my studies. I'll give it everything I've got, filling the stretching holes in my heart with the passion and purpose Maxime so charitably offered me.

"Fuck, Zoe." His fingers tighten on my nipple, twisting not to hurt but because lost as we are in the midst of this new phase of our forced relationship, he's forgetting his own strength. "If you don't want me to pummel your ass, you have to tell me now. Don't tease me, little flower."

No. I want the dirty. I want the reminder of who I am. I need to remember this wanton woman on her knees is all I'll ever be so that I'll never want things I can't have again. It hurts too damn much.

"Goddamn, Zoe. You're killing me." He kisses my shoulder and starts pulling out.

I reach behind me to grip his wrist. "Give it to me, Maxime."

He hesitates.

"Give it to me, damn you."

"Why?" he asks in a hoarse voice.

"Because I need it too."

Stroking a palm up my spine, he offers tenderness in an advance exchange for the violence we both crave. "I've got you, *cherie*."

In this, he does. On a physical level, he's the king. Gripping my hips, he enters me slowly, taking his time until his groin is pressed against my ass, but that's all the concession he gives me before he lets go. We're rough. He gives me what I need and takes what he wants. Despite *last night* and everything it signifies, despite the endless orgasms, I beg him to make me come.

It's a vicious circle I can't escape. I'll hate him now and be back on my knees tonight, begging him to fill me with the token of his ownership. His name whispers over my lips in a frantic cry as he rubs my clit and makes me explode before spilling his release in my body.

I collapse onto my stomach when my arms give out. Maxime follows me down, keeping his cock buried in my body and his weight on his elbows. He presses kisses and sweet words on my ear, praising me for how well I've taken him.

I'm already lethargic again. It's hard to keep my eyes open. Needing something—someone—to hold onto, I fold my fingers around his hand that rests next to my face. At the hiss of air he sucks through his teeth, I open my eyes. The tip of his index finger sports a nasty, red scab. It looks like a burn.

Lifting my shoulders off the mattress, I turn his finger toward the light for a better look. "Maxime! What happened?"

He pulls away. "Nothing."

I wince at the bite of pain when he frees his cock.

"Did that happen in the fight?" I ask, rolling onto my side to face him. I hadn't noticed it last night, but I've been so wrought out it's possible I missed his injuries.

His laugh is cold. "There was no fight."

Pushing off me, he gets up. "Have a shower with me. I need to go shortly."

My mood darkens. "Business? Now?"

"Yes," he replies in a clipped tone.

Instead of pushing the matter, I let him pull me to my feet.

He washes me in the shower and insists on drying my hair with the hairdryer afterward as if he's scared I'll catch a cold and my death with it. We dress and have an early dinner together. Francine's eyes are red-rimmed from crying. Maxime doesn't comment, and I don't ask, assuming it's because of worry over what could've happened to him.

"Isn't it weird to keep an ex-lover around?" I ask when she's gone.

He shrugs. "It was sex. Now it's over. There's nothing weird about that."

Right.

"You better have an early night," he says. "It'll do you good."

After the main meal, he excuses himself. I follow him to the entrance where he pulls on a jacket and coat, but he's withdrawn again, already preoccupied with the business and the fires I imagine he had to put out after last night. When the door shuts behind him, I can't help but stand in the middle of the foyer with my arms wrapped around myself, feeling lost. I can't help but think that every time he walks out of the door he may never come back.

CHAPTER 11

Zoe

The minute my back hits the mattress, I pass out. I have no idea if Maxime came to bed, because I sleep nine hours straight, and when I wake in the morning, I'm alone. It's still early. Part of me is worried and part of me grateful for the space. My emotions are all over the place. I'm tearful, and my defenses are down. That makes me vulnerable—a susceptible target for more hurt. I need to pull myself together.

I try not to think, but the gears won't stop turning in my head. Where is Maxime? How is Gautier's family coping? Are the police going after Maxime for the killings? Will I ever get away from my captor now? Do I *want* to get away? Can I really turn a blind eye to everything and throw myself into my studies even if I don't deserve a place in the program?

The questions are futile, because the answers, even if I had them, won't change anything. Very little is in my control. By the time I've showered and dressed, I don't feel lighter. The killings and truth Maxime revealed still weigh heavily on my chest.

I go down for breakfast, walking down the dim hallway with the portraits. The faces stare at me, judging quietly. A man died. Several. Some by my kidnapper's hand. How does one live with that? How does *he*? The stairs creak under my feet. The noise is amplified in the big, quiet house. I pass empty rooms and the cold library and stop in front of the locked study door. The phones must be in there together with everything else Maxime doesn't want me to find. It's useless, but I feel the handle. As I expected, the door doesn't swing open under my pressure.

I continue to the dining room. Fruit and croissants are set out on the table. Giving the buttery pastries and fat oranges a long look, I go on, walking to the kitchen. What I need is comfort food. Familiar food.

When I enter, Francine looks up from wiping down the counters. My presence makes her go stiff. I don't bother to say good morning, as I don't expect her to reply. Going past her, I take a mug from the cupboard.

"Can I help you?" she asks, propping her hands on her hips.

"No, thanks."

Her mouth presses into a thin line when I pour myself a cup of coffee. "Don't you drink tea? It's in the cupboard behind you."

"Not today." I blow on the brew. "Oh, was the coffee for you?"

She dumps the cleaning cloth on the counter. "I'll just have to make a fresh pot."

"There's still plenty left."

Grabbing the flask, she pours what's left of the coffee down the drain and rinses it. I take a sip. It's strong. While she polishes the flask harder than necessary with a dishcloth, I look for the sugar. All I find is a box with a corner cut open. Since there isn't a sugar pot, I fill a cup.

"Oh, for God's sake." She pushes a bowl with cubes my way. "This is France. Get used to the way we do things here."

I consider that for a moment. It's a stupid rebellion, childish really.

On any other day, I may not have found her rebuke worthy of a response, but today isn't just another day. Today, I add two heaped spoons of sugar to my coffee, giving her a sweet smile. Her fingers clench on the dishcloth. Making a mental note to never take cubes, I pop a slice of bread into the toaster. What is it with the French and cubes, anyway?

Eyeing the bread, she says, "There *is* breakfast in the dining room." She continues, adding a little jab, "As per Max's orders."

"Does he decide what I'm eating?"

"He pays my salary." Her lips curve into a smile. "That means whatever he decides goes."

I lean my butt against the cupboard. "Exactly. That makes him your boss. So, if I were you, I'd remember my place."

Her eyes flare. "That makes you what? His *girlfriend*?"

The toast pops. I dump it on a plate. "Oh, nothing as romantic as that. I think until yesterday I was a hostage. Today, apparently, the term is property."

She blanches. She doesn't like the statement. That's strange. To me, property sounds like an insult.

"I suppose hoping there's peanut butter is stretching it too far?" I ask as I go through the food cupboards.

"You're nothing but a distraction," she says to my back. "Max is never that careless. You almost got him killed last night."

Inwardly, I still at the words. It's not as if it hasn't been running through my mind. Anyone can die at any moment, but Max's lifestyle puts him—us—at a higher risk. A *much* higher risk.

I settle on the butter and jam in the fridge.

"Don't you have anything to say?" she asks.

"I'll pass your concern to Maxime."

I've lost my appetite, but I spread a thick layer of butter and jam on the toast and take a seat by the window nook to eat.

"Do you mind?" she asks just as I open my mouth to take a bite. "I'm busy, and you're in the way."

She's asking to me leave? I lower my hand. "Actually, I do mind." I don't know where the nastiness comes from. I only know I've reached my limit. "I'd like to eat in peace. You can come back in fifteen minutes."

Color rises in her cheeks as she stares at me with her wide green eyes so perfectly set off against her porcelain white skin.

"If you prefer that the order comes directly from your *boss*," I say when she doesn't move, "you can always call *Max*."

"Your days are numbered." The color of her irises turns brilliant. "We'll see who'll have the last laugh." Head held high, she walks from the kitchen.

If only she knew. Even if Damian's life is no longer the sword Maxime holds over my head, he made it clear he won't let me go. Anyway, running is impossible. I have no money, no passport, and I doubt I'll get far, not if Maxime is the head of the most powerful mafia group in France. I can dial no one except for Maxime from my phone, and I don't have access to a laptop. The only measure of freedom I have is going to school. Phones aren't allowed in class, and Maxime's men are watching my every move outside of class. Even if I did get my hands on a phone or somehow managed to send an email to the South African embassy, Maxime made it clear he'd chase me. After what happened in South Africa, I don't doubt it for a minute. Damian is in jail, unable to help me. I don't have friends or allies here. I can't ask anyone for help.

Even if I wanted to get away, I'm stuck.

Despondency descends on me. I need to get out of this house. After rinsing my mug and plate, I grab my satchel and step outside. Two cars are waiting. Benoit drives me to school while three men follow in the second car. I don't make a fuss. If anything, I'm grateful. I'm scared, but I can't lock myself up and hide from Maxime's enemies forever. Clutching my satchel, I look around for cars with tinted windows as we enter the city. I'm nervous. The tension snakes up my stomach and squeezes my chest.

"You can relax," Benoit says. "We cleaned the streets up."

I glance at him. "I'm really sorry about Gautier."

His jaw bunches.

"I'll understand if you think it's my fault," I say.

"I'm not an idiot."

"That's not what I said."

"Look, it's bad enough that I have to babysit you. Can we please not talk? I'm not exactly in the mood for conversation. If not for you —" He cuts off with a cussword, then swears some more under his breath.

I shrug. "Sure." The nonchalant act costs me. It takes everything I have not to show him how guilty his words make me feel. It's easier to roll the window down and pretend I'm staring outside.

Sighing, he wipes a hand over his beard. "Look, I've got nothing against you—"

"You don't have to explain. I understand."

When he parks in front of the school, I get out before he does. "Thanks for the ride," I say before shutting the door.

I'm early, but when I arrive at the classroom, Madame Page and the other students are already there.

I pull out a chair next to Thérèse, and whisper, "I thought the class started at nine."

"It does." She gives me a bleary-eyed look. "Some of us aren't lucky enough to get a free ride. We're all putting additional time in and working extra hard to pass."

"Mademoiselle Hart?" Madame Page calls from the front. "A word with you outside, please."

All heads turn to me when I follow Madame Page outside. Benoit and one of the guards stand a short distance down the hallway. Madame Page startles at their presence. With their suits and dark glasses, there's no guessing as to who or what they are, and what they're doing here.

Ignoring them with visible effort, she shuts the classroom door and pushes her glasses over her head. "You may think you don't have to attend classes like everyone else, but I won't allow you to make an idiot of me and a joke of my course."

"I'm really sorry I wasn't here yesterday. I know it reflects poorly on me, especially since it was only the second day, but I assure you I'm very serious about this course. My absence was due to circumstances beyond my control."

"Circumstances, mm?" Her look is sour. "That's your excuse?"

"It's not an excuse."

"Then care to tell me why you didn't grace us with your presence?"

"I... Um, personal reasons."

"Personal reasons." She purses her lips. "If this was anyone else, they would've been expelled." She points a finger at me. "No absence without a doctor's certificate. The fact that you're here means someone else lost out on an opportunity, someone talented and willing to work. If you can't appreciate what's been given to you on a silver platter, at least try to respect the rules."

"I'm sorry. I really am." I can't even say it won't happen again, because my life isn't in my own hands. Maxime decides. He controls my days, nights, hours, and minutes.

She drops her glasses back over her eyes. "Apology not accepted. Get inside and try not to disrupt the rest of the class, especially not Thérèse. She's on the bottom of the ladder. If she can't beat five of her fellow students, she's out. Are we clear?"

"Yes," I say, averting my eyes.

Embarrassment heats my cheeks as I follow her back inside, but I ignore the stares and arrange my pencils and sketchpad on the table. For the rest of the morning, I try to catch up on what I've missed. They've completed the first model on business theory. Even if practical isn't until next year, all of them have brought in pieces for Madame Page's feedback. That was what the others were working on until late last night. I'm a good seamstress with three years of experience, but I realize with a sinking heart they're all better than me. If I'm to keep up, I'll have to work at home. I'll have to work harder and longer hours. I don't have a choice but to use the sewing machine Maxime gave me, even if I was adamant about not touching it after finding out how I got into the school.

Madame Page announces a group project where we're supposed to work in teams of two to hand-dye an organic textile for our textile science class. There's a lot of excited whispering about it. Some of the girls already call out one another's names to pair in teams.

At lunchtime, Benoit and the other guy follow me to the canteen where I grab a sandwich and fruit salad. They get the cooked lunch, pay for their meals and mine, and sit down at a table in the corner. I doubt they'll appreciate my presence, so I approach Christine, the pretty dark-haired girl.

"May I?" I motion at the empty seat next to her.

She blows a sigh from the corner of her mouth. "I don't own the tables or the chairs. You can sit wherever you want."

"Do you want to work together on the team project?" I ask as I sit down.

"Work together?" She laughs. "With you?"

I unwrap my sandwich. "It could be fun."

She snorts. "No, thanks."

The rejection stings a little, but I'm the one who has to put more effort into getting on with my fellow students. I understand why they're mad. I can't give up that easily. "Why not?"

Her fork clanks as she puts it down on her plate. "Why not?"

"Yes," I say, taking a bite from the baguette.

"Here's why. You don't have to work. You don't have to earn this degree. Hell, you don't even have to show up. You'll graduate with flying colors, open an exclusive brand label with a head office on the Riviera that your rich mafia boyfriend pays for, and because you're null and worthless at designing but like to pretend that you're a hotshot fashion guru, you'll pay people like me who worked my ass off to work for you.

"My designs will be branded with your label, and you and your shady boyfriend will carry on drinking champagne with the high society and making more money while I work my fingers to the bone, get paid your peanuts, and watch as you take all the credit. That's fucking why."

It takes me a moment to find words. "Is that what you think of me?"

"That's how it works, sunshine." Picking up her tray, she gets to her feet. "Excuse me if I'm not exactly in the mood for teaming up with you."

"You don't know me. You have no right judging me."

"I have every right. My father works three jobs to pay for my studies. I would've worked six if I didn't have to study day and night. We don't get things handed to us. We earn it." She adds with a sneer, "You won't understand what that means."

"Maybe I understand more than what you give me credit for. Maybe if you give me a chance—"

"Don't you get it? I don't *want* to give you a chance."

Aware of everyone staring, I keep my voice low. "Surely, we all deserve a chance."

"You want me to spell it out for you? Even if your work didn't suck, you'd still be a fake."

The tightness in my stomach grows. "What do you mean my work sucks?"

"Madame Page presented our profiles yesterday while you were playing hooky. Grow up. You're not a princess, and this isn't the eighties. Frills and lace are long since out of fashion. Your designs are cheesy and immature. You're only making a fool of yourself." Giving me a pitiful shake of her head, she walks to the table next to ours. "Can I please sit somewhere I won't get indigestion?"

The girls move up to make space. Someone takes her tray while she comes back for her chair. It makes a screeching sound as she drags it over the floor to her new place. The dining room has gone quiet. Everyone is looking at me.

I bite into my sandwich and chew like I don't care. I swallow like the food isn't a lump of sawdust in my throat that threatens to choke me. From the corner of my eye, I see Benoit wipe his mouth and dump the napkin on the tray. When he pushes back his chair, I give him a small shake of my head. Interfering, and God forbid forcing Christine to sit with me, will only make matters worse. I eat in silence while the people around me go back to their conversations. Their whispers are quieter than before, their gazes often colliding with mine. They don't even bother to look away when I catch them staring.

This is the moment I hit rock bottom, when the day just gets too much. Finishing off the last of the sandwich, I swallow it down with some water and brush the crumbs from my skirt. I grab my bag and walk outside into the heat where I can drag in the salty sea air and bite the inside of my cheek until the urge to cry passes.

Benoit and his buddy come out of the building. I turn my back on them so they won't see the humiliation on my face. God, I could do with a friend right now. In a life that was still my own, I would've called one of the girls from work, and we'd be binge watching a silly series while pigging out on popcorn and wine. Or we would've sewn together, creating *frilly* and *cheesy* creations that are immature and out of fashion. I inhale deeply to steady myself.

Taking my phone from my bag, I stare at it for a long time before I dial Maxime's number.

His deep, rich timbre comes over the line. "This is a pleasant surprise." The way he rolls the R still makes the hairs in the nape of my neck stand on end in both a good and bad way. "A first for us."

I've never called him. He seems pleased that I've finally relented. Now that I'm speaking to him, I hesitate. Maybe this isn't a good idea. "Am I bothering you?"

"Never." I can almost hear him smile. "To what do I owe the unexpected pleasure?"

I study the drops from the wet grass on the tip of my shoe. "Did you come to bed last night?"

His voice turns even deeper. "Why? Did you miss me?"

I bite my lip. Always, but he doesn't need to know that. "I was just wondering."

"Just wondering, huh?"

"Yes," I say, kicking at a stone.

"Were you worried about me, Zoe?" From the satisfaction that sounds in his tone, he already thinks I did. He just wants me to admit it.

Suddenly, I'm too tired for this game. I'm too tired to hide my feelings from him. "How could I not be?" I don't bring up the other night again. We've spoken about it as much as is healthy for both of us.

His manner sobers. "I didn't want to make you worry. I had loose ends to tie up."

"So, you didn't sleep." I glance up to catch Benoit studying me. "You must be tired."

"Don't worry, I can go a couple of nights without sleeping. Is this why you're calling? You want to know if I'm tired?" He adds in a huskier voice, "Or you'd like to see me?"

The hope in his words almost makes me give in, but no, that's not why I'm calling. I'm still too unsettled and angry. I'm upset that I even have to make this call to ask his permission.

"Zoe, what is it?"

I take a deep breath. "I'd like to meet Sylvie for coffee after class."

There's a short hesitation. "You would?"

I drill my shoe into the spongy grass, my stomach hard with the expectation of a negative answer. "You said you didn't mind."

"I didn't think you wanted to see my family again."

"Sylvie's nice," I offer as a weak explanation. I don't want to tell him about what happened today. I don't want to fight about it again. It will remind me of the night—*Stop it!* Harping on it does *not* help.

"Zoe."

"Yes?"

"You don't need my permission to have coffee with Sylvie. As long as you tell me where you're going and take my men with you."

His answer bowls me over. It's not what I expected. "Really?"

"Absolutely. Go out with her and have fun."

My mouth drops open. It's almost too good to be true. "Um, okay?" I frown, fumbling for words. "Can I call Sylvie from Benoit's phone? Does he have her number?"

"You don't have to use Benoit's phone. I added Sylvie's number to your caller list."

"Thank you." I guess?

"Send me a text to let me know where you're going."

"Right, so you know if you shouldn't come fetch me." Hastily, I add, "In case you were going to. I mean, *if* she's available."

He chuckles. "That'll be considerate."

"I'll let you get back to work, then." Or rather his shady criminalities.

"I'll miss you." He waits a beat. When I say nothing, he hangs up.

I check my watch. It's almost time to go back inside, but I can fit a quick call in. When I check my caller list, Sylvie's number is already there. I press dial.

"Hi," I say when she answers. "It's Zoe."

"Oh, hi." She sounds upbeat. "I'm so glad you called."

I'm a little uncomfortable. Maybe I'm putting her out. "Are you back in Paris yet?"

"The university starts in a month."

Gathering my courage, I press on. "That coffee you mentioned, does the offer still stand?"

She gives a small laugh. "Of course."

"Are you available today?" I ask, holding my breath.

"Sure," she says after a beat. "Where would you like to meet?"

"You tell me." My voice is lighter with relief. "I'm still new to Marseille."

"Where are you?"

"At school. I get off at six."

"Okay. I'll text you an address."

We say our goodbyes just as the lunch break is over. Students who've been lazing on the lawn stream back into the building. They're all younger than me, maybe eighteen or nineteen, fresh out of school. I definitely don't belong here.

Benoit comes over, handing me my satchel. "You forgot this."

"Thanks." I don't look at him. "I better get back inside."

"Those girls," he says as I start walking, "they have no business treating you like this."

Stopping, I meet his gaze. "I don't know what you're talking about."

He gives me a narrowed look. "I heard what she said to you. Everyone did."

"Well, maybe I deserved that." Seriously, how are they supposed to feel about having me on board because my mafia *boyfriend* forced it?

"They need to be put back in place."

"Don't say anything to Maxime. It'll only make the situation worse."

He regards me stoically.

"Please, Benoit. Don't make this harder for me than what it already is."

Still no answer.

I can't delay much longer without being late for class. Taking a shortcut over the grass, I head for my building.

CHAPTER 12

Maxime

The last time I visited Dr. Delphine Bisset was before my trip to South Africa. She's a good shrink. I'm not the self-searching or inwardly reflecting kind, but she helped me understand shitloads about myself, which, believe it or not, is imperative in my business. You can't know your enemies if you don't know yourself. Delphine is the only one with the balls to be honest with me. The psychiatrist I tried before her told me whatever I wanted to hear. I guess he was worried I'd shoot him.

Pushing the door to her uptown consultation room open, I walk to the receptionist's desk. I'm alone. My guards don't tag along for this. My visits to the shrink are something I prefer to keep private. My enemies may take it for a weakness.

The girl looks up. Her easy smile vanishes. "Good morning, sir." Her hand is already on the phone. "Dr. Bisset is with a patient, but I'll let her know you're here."

I give her a polite nod and take a seat among the other waiting patients. Five minutes later, the door to the office opens and a young man exits in front of Delphine.

"Max." She offers me a warm smile and beckons me with a wave.

The other patients glare at me when I stand. I don't have an appointment.

Ignoring their nasty looks, Delphine shuts the door and shakes my hand. "It's been a while."

"I've been busy."

"Naturally," she says with wit. "Crime will do that to you." Walking to the informal sitting area, she motions for me to take a seat. "What brings you today?"

I sit down in one of the armchairs and adjust my jacket. "A woman."

"Ah." She takes the seat opposite me and crosses her legs. "You mean one you've seen more than twice?"

"Six months, actually."

She tilts her head. "Very out of character for you. What makes this one different?"

"She's innocent. Pure. I suppose you could say she's naïve."

Folding her hands, she studies me. "You're attracted to these *innocent* traits?"

"Naturally," I say, quoting her earlier remark. "Opposites attract and all that."

Her smile is eloquent. "Why?"

"She's everything I'm not. I'd say that's obvious."

"How is this a problem for you?" she asks in her smooth voice.

Leaning forward, I rest my elbows on my knees and tip my fingers together. I give her a long look as I weigh my words. Their heaviness bears down right in the center of my chest. "Am I capable of love, Doctor?"

"Max." She blows out a short sigh. It's a soft sound laced with compassion. "In order to love, you need to have empathy."

"Whenever I'm the cause of her pain, I hurt myself worse than what she's hurting."

"You're inflicting pain on yourself?"

"Yes."

"As punishment?"

"As a reminder."

"To have empathy?"

"Yes."

"Physical pain doesn't replace compassion, Max. Compassion comes from the heart."

"That's the thing. She makes me feel." I press a palm over my chest where the dead skin crawls from the mere thought of her. "She makes me feel *things*."

"Define things."

"Fear. Fucking loads of it. Weakness. She makes me care."

"Can you put her first, above your own needs?"

I consider that. Putting Zoe first will mean doing what's best for her and what she wants—to let her go. Only, I can't do that, and it has nothing to do with her brother's diamonds. I'll never set her free. She's mine. *Mine*. I fucking claimed her. I took her virginity. I came inside her. No, I'm afraid letting her go has and will never be an option. Tilting my head back, I scrub a hand over my face.

"Do you manipulate her, Max?"

I look back at the doctor. "For her own good."

"Do you lie to her?"

"When I must."

"Do you feel shame or remorse for your lies and manipulations?"

"No."

Her small smile is sad, conveying a wordless message.

"Yeah, yeah." I rake my fingers through my hair. "I'm still the pathologically lying, manipulative, coldhearted prick with the versatile criminal behavior and lack of moral judgment."

"And high intelligence," she adds, "not to mention ruthlessness."

"That's supposed to help me?"

She leans her arms on her knees. "You're the most ruthless person I know, meaning you're willing to take risks. Are you willing to take a risk for her and step out of your comfort zone? You're also a clever man, a man who knows how his behavior impacts others, even if you don't feel guilty about it. You want to do better. That's why you sought me out for starters."

"Even if I do better, I'll still be the fucking psychopath incapable of love."

"You suffer from emotional detachment, but feeling something is a beginning. We can work with that."

Frustration mounts. "I'm pretty much agitated right now. That counts for an emotion."

"Your frustration and anger are manifestations of your selfish impatience. We've already covered this."

"Isn't caring for someone love in its own kind of way?"

"It depends on the root of the caring. Is this about her or you?"

I shift in my seat. "What do you mean?"

"Do you care because of how being with her makes *you* feel, or do you care about how she feels, regardless of yourself?"

"I don't want her to be sad or unhappy."

"How do you feel when she's unhappy?"

"Frightened."

"Why?"

"That it'll slip away."

"That what will slip away?"

"Her. This. What I'm feeling when she's around."

"Right." She raises a brow. "So, this is about you."

"I love my family, don't I?"

"You hate your father, and your brother is your biggest enemy. You have a sense of responsibility toward your mother, and you experience feelings of injustice for your father's behavior, but you lack the empathy that forms unconditional relationships with your family."

"This woman—*my* woman—grew up in a dysfunctional family in a poor neighborhood. She's been exposed to every circumstance you quoted for making a psychopath, yet she's not like me. How come?"

"Max." She sighs again. "It's not a secret you can steal. Every person's internal and external factors are unique. As I've told you before, I suspect in your case it's a combination of your violent circumstances and genetic inheritance."

"So," I say with a wry smile, "you're telling me I'll never be able to love."

"I think you do love in your own way, and I do believe you'll be able to build a trusting and sharing relationship if you can manage to see things from your partner's perspective."

"But?"

"But in this case, your care is selfish. You said it yourself. She gives you what you don't have. You're opposites. You're using her to balance yourself."

Great. This helps a fucking lot, and it changes nothing.

"Thank you, Doctor."

"Always a pleasure, Max." Despite her strict no touching policy, she leans over and squeezes my hand. "I'm here when you need me."

I stand. "I appreciate your time."

"No, you don't." Her intelligent eyes meet mine. "You expect it. In fact, you insist." Not unkindly, she adds, "Next time, try to be considerate to everyone else and make an appointment."

She's right, as always.

I'd give my life to give Zoe the love she deserves, but I am what I am.

I leave Dr. Bisset's office still the same man, a man unable to reciprocate love.

CHAPTER 13

Zoe

As promised, Sylvie sends me a text, suggesting a brasserie in the old town.

Benoit drives me while the men from this morning follow again. With the yellow awning and red window frames, the brasserie looks like a typical French postcard. Before, I would've thought this a dream. Now I can only admire the image abstractly, a deeper part of me hating everything associated with this city.

Loud chatter greets me when I push the door open. The inside smells of coffee and beer. It's busy. People sipping wine or espresso occupy the tables. Not one is free. It seems like a popular place to meet for drinks after work.

Benoit follows behind me and then overtakes to greet some of the customers. I spot Sylvie at the bar. She's wearing a fitted powder-blue dress with a short jacket and ballerina flats. The ensemble is simple but stylish. It's the kind of understated elegance Madame Page and

Maxime's mother favor. Noelle and Hadrienne, too. This is the French bourgeois style.

Benoit raises a hand to catch the bartender's attention. The bartender smiles kindly when he notices me. He says something to Sylvie, who turns.

"There you are," she says when I reach her, kissing my cheeks. She holds me at arm's length to study my leggings and off-shoulder jersey. "You look gorgeous."

I love this jersey. It has pirate sleeves and a drawstring in the hem for a puffy look. "Thank you."

"Come." She takes my hand and leads me to the back. "Let's sit."

The men at the table for which she's headed get up when they see us, take their drinks, and leave.

"That's very gentlemanly," I say.

"Ha. Don't you believe that. It's only because they know who Papa is. Espresso?"

"Tea, please."

She signals the bartender, making a C and a T with her hands. "So, what made you call?"

A man died saving my life. My kidnapper went after the attackers and killed them. Not only did I discover that said kidnapper is a mafia boss, but also that he deceived me when he held my brother's life over my head. I threatened him with an icepick. He tied me up and punished me with multiple orgasms all day. My teacher and classmates think I'm a fake and hate me. I won't even know where to begin. There's no way I can answer her question honestly.

"It's tough," she says, covering my hand with hers, "but you can't let it get to you."

I force myself back to the moment. "What?"

"The shooting. You can't let them win."

"Who?"

"*Brise de Mer.*"

"Is that a gang?"

"The Corsicans. They've been at war with my family for years."

The bartender arrives with our drinks. He serves them with ginger cookies and leaves.

How does Sylvie cope with mafia life? How can she sit there so unafraid, looking so normal? "I don't know how you can live like this."

"Don't worry." She lifts her cup to her lips. "Our men will take care of us."

I consider her words. They strike a chord of irony. "It's funny. I used to have this stupid fantasy of being saved from my miserable life and carried off to a happy ending by a knight in shining armor. Now I don't like that fantasy so much. I didn't like being *saved*." I make quotation marks with my fingers. I can't tell her *saved* is a sarcastic term for kidnapped. "I think I prefer to be in control of my life."

"Oh, honey." She makes a sad face. "The women belonging to the *family* have very little freedom, but we do have control. You just have to be clever about it."

"You mean manipulation?"

She cocks a shoulder. "Papa wouldn't let Noelle and me study, so we got *depressed*." She chuckles. "We started eating so much Maman told Papa no man would ever marry us if we couldn't even fit into a wedding dress."

"That made him agree?"

"Papa's biggest fear is that we won't give him grandchildren."

A life of constant manipulation seems awfully sad, not to mention exhausting, but I'm not going to insult her by telling her so.

"You need to figure out what Max's weak points are," she continues. "You, for one, seem to be a pretty strong weakness. Surely, you must have some bargaining power in bed."

My cheeks heat.

"See?" She wags her eyebrows. "I knew I was right. You need to convince him to let you come visit me in Paris. We'll go out and do some shopping. It'll make you feel a whole lot better."

It's appealing, but a crazy idea. "I doubt that'll ever happen."

"You may be surprised. Max cares about you. He wants you to be happy. I'm sure he'll do anything to make sure you are. He may come along to Paris and bring an army with him, but he'd do that if you go about it the right way."

The right way. He's showed me time and again he'd treat me kindly if I behave, but that's just another form of manipulation, and I'm so tired of the games. I just want to be free. I want to make my own decisions and determine my own actions. I don't want to have hidden agendas. I want to give because I care, not because I need something in return. How can I explain that to Sylvie who's been raised to navigate this world and its myriad of landmines?

"We have to make the best of what we have," Sylvie says, pushing her empty cup aside. "Accept what we can't change. Let's face it, we have it a lot better than many other women." She gets to her feet. "Do you mind if I have a cigarette?"

"Of course not."

She grabs her bag. "You'll have to come with me. I'll have to smoke in the toilet." When I frown, she says, "Papa doesn't know."

"Oh." Of course. The people here all know Benoit. That means they all know the *family*. One of the men will see it as his duty to inform Sylvie's father if she lights up a cigarette in the street.

When I follow her to the bathroom, Benoit takes up a position by the bar from where he can keep an eye on the door. It's a unisex bathroom. The space is cramped with a small basin on one side and a toilet on the other.

She locks the door and takes a cigarette from her purse. "I can't buy a packet, or Papa will know. Every tobacco shop owner in Marseille pays Papa rent."

"Then how do you get them?" I ask, leaning on the counter.

"Some of the guards are friendly." She takes a drag and blows out a thin line of smoke. "I know which ones won't talk. See? You just have to be clever."

I both admire and pity Sylvie. I pity her lack of freedom and admire her survival skills. I admire her outlook on all of this. I wish I could cope so easily. I study her from under my lashes. Can I trust her? She did open up to me about forcing her father's hand to let her study and smoking behind his back, and she was kind enough to make time and meet me.

"Can I ask you something, Sylvie?"

She blows smoke from the corner of her mouth. "Shoot."

"What's the difference between a mistress and property?"

"Where did you hear about that?" She offers me the cigarette.

I shake my head. "Just something the guys talked about."

"A mistress is a lover. It means an open-ended relationship that continues for however long the guy wants."

"What about what the woman wants?"

"In our world, honey, it's always the guy who decides when to call it quits. Property, on the other hand, is a dead end. It means a man has claimed a woman for life. It's like being a mistress, only forever."

The revelation shouldn't shock me. Maxime said as much when he told me he'd never let me go. Still, her explanation settles like an iron ball in my stomach.

She scrutinizes me with shrewd eyes. "Did Max tell you you're property?"

I can't even answer that.

Her smile is sympathetic. "Give him a chance, Zoe. Max isn't that bad. You do feel for him, don't you?"

Placing a hand on my forehead, I say, "I don't even know what I feel anymore."

"It's obvious you care. What are you so worried about?"

"It's complicated."

"Tell him how you feel."

Chewing my lip, I consider that. "I don't know."

"Look, you're stuck, anyway. What can it hurt?"

I inhale deeply. "That's the problem. It can hurt."

"Max really is crazy about you. He's different with you. Just give it a shot. If you don't try, you'll never know." Waving a hand to disperse the smoke, she puts the cigarette out in the sink and drops the butt in the trashcan. "We better get back before they wonder what's taking us so long."

"They? You have men following you, too?"

"Protecting me." She winks. Going through her bag, she takes out an anti-tobacco spray and applies it liberally to her clothes and hair before popping a chewing gum into her mouth. "There. Ready to go?"

I nod.

"You'll be okay. Trust me." She takes my hand. "Promise we'll do this again."

I can't help but smile. "I promise."

"Good." She kisses my cheek. "You can do with a friend."

A man in a suit I don't recognize stands next to Benoit when we exit.

He addresses Sylvie when we reach them. "What took so long?"

She bats her eyelashes. "Period. Changing tampons and all that. Want more details?"

The man coughs. Benoit looks away. She gives me a smile that says, *see?*

She's as trapped as I am. It's an eye opener. I feel sorry for her, but I also feel a little lighter when Benoit drives me home. Sylvie has helped me face a truth, something I've known in my heart for a while but couldn't admit. My love for Maxime isn't conventional. Our relationship isn't healthy or smooth sailing. He's a hardened criminal with a dark heart, and I'm a naïve romantic with an abandoned princess fantasy. Somehow, we work together. Somehow, we've rubbed off on each other. We're diamonds in the rough, cutting our edges together. I no longer want to leave. This is crazy, the craziest thing I've ever done, but I'm going to tell Maxime how I feel. I want to try, because maybe, just maybe, there are ways to survive Maxime, and maybe I don't have to do it alone.

CHAPTER 14

Maxime

When Benoit calls me while Zoe is having coffee with Sylvie and tells me what has happened at school, I'm fucking fuming. I leave my father's office earlier than usual and drive to the campus, bargaining on the fact that Madame Page always works late.

She's alone in her office when I enter just before seven.

"Can I help you?" she asks with her head bent over some sketches and a cigarette dangling from her mouth.

"You most definitely can," I say, striding to her desk.

Her paper-thin skin turns white when she looks up. "Mr. Belshaw."

Yeah. She should be scared.

Her hand shakes as she tips the ash. "I'm busy."

I turn a chair around and straddle it. "Let's get something straight. Zoe deserves to be here the same as everyone else. She has more passion in her style than that shift dress with the fancy label you're wearing. If she's not in class, it's because I need her to be elsewhere. Do you understand?"

Her lip curls. "You're being very clear."

"Good."

"However, this is a serious establishment. I won't let you intimidate me."

I grin. "Let me remind you that the women who earn enough money to afford your label move in the same circles. It'll be a pity if their eyes are opened as to just how undeserving your style is of praise."

Her right eye twitches.

"Is that enough intimidation for you?" I ask. "I can get as persuasive as you'd like me to be."

"Quite enough," she says with a tight jaw.

"Great." I rap my knuckles on her desk. "I'd hate to destroy your career when you're so close to retiring." I get up. "Nice talking to you."

I leave with a smile.

AT HOME, I find Zoe sitting on her favorite bench in the garden, sipping a glass of wine and staring at the sea. I study her profile to make out her mood, but for once her expression doesn't give much away. Her gaze is trained on the distance, her thoughts seeming far-off.

"How was school?" I ask when I stop next to her, observing her closely.

She looks up at me with a start. "Good."

I know why she asked Benoit to keep his mouth shut. After all, it's my fault they all hate her. Perhaps I should've been upfront about how she'd gotten into the school, but she was just so damn excited about it. Her joy made me feel things I've never felt before. It made me *happy*. I just didn't have the heart to disappoint her.

Tracing the curve of her shoulder with a finger, I ask, "How was your coffee date with Sylvie?"

Her face brightens a little. "We had a good time."

"I'm glad."

I mean it. Despite what she thinks, her unhappiness affects me. I don't like it when she's lonely or sad. The attempt on her life still hangs over us. So does everything else that has happened—the icepick incident, coming inside her, tying her up, punishing her…and telling her the truth. The air hasn't been cleared, and all this pollution makes it hard to go back to how we used to be. Then again, do I want to go back? Perhaps this is a step forward.

Tentatively, she lifts a hand. Ever so slowly, she cups my fingers where they rest on her shoulder. I don't breathe. I don't even blink for the fear that she'll move her hand away. Joy surges through my chest. Such a small gesture, yet such a big step in bridging this gap that has fallen between us since the attempt on her life. We stay like this for the longest time as I try to understand this olive branch she's offering. Did Sylvie manage to talk some sense into her?

Fran breaks the spell, calling, "Dinner is ready."

Bloody hell. I turn on her. "You hardly have to announce it."

She pales and wilts. "The food will get cold."

My voice rises with impatience. "Leave it where you always do. In the warm drawer."

"It's all right." Zoe gets to her feet. "We're coming." When my fingers tighten on her shoulder, she adds quickly, "I'm hungry."

I know what Zoe is doing. She's trying to prevent a fight. It's working. My body goes slack, and the earlier tranquility we've somehow found flows back through my veins.

Fran turns away with a wounded expression.

"I think she has feelings for you," Zoe says when Fran is out of earshot.

"Our relationship is strictly professional." Gripping her chin, I note the dark rings under her eyes. "Maybe we should have an early night."

"I can't. I missed a lot in class yesterday. I have to catch up."

I trace her bottom lip with my thumb. "Not at the expense of your health. You need your rest."

"Maxime, stop babying me." She swallows, then glances away. When she looks back at me, she says in a composed tone, "I need this."

"I know you do, *cherie*." Ah, hell. My resolve crumbles. "I'll sit up with you. I won't be able to sleep, anyway." Not if she's not in my bed.

"Honestly, you don't have to."

"No, I don't." In a rare instant, I give her the truth. "I want to."

CHAPTER 15

Maxime

For the next few days, clearing the city of infiltrators dominates my time. I flush out the disloyal men and dole out deaths as examples and punishment where due. It's not only about survival. It's also about keeping the streets safe for the people we protect and the businesses that rely on us.

The attack on Zoe's life left me edgy. Volatile. Even Leonardo stays out of my way. My instincts scream at me to lock her up again, but I understand enough of human nature to know it'll be a mistake. Zoe needs the illusion of freedom. She needs her friendship with Sylvie. She needs to go to classes and chase her dream. I want to own her, not crush her. I want her to flourish, because I need her for who she is. Because of this, when she comes to me one night in the library after I returned home late and another dinner we didn't eat together, I'm attentive to her needs.

"How was your day?" she asks, handing me a whiskey.

She's been nothing but exemplary, a good little girl, and it earns her my kindness. Zoe isn't my enemy. I have no desire to harm or hurt her. I neither take pleasure from teaching her lessons, nor from inflicting pain on myself when I'm hurting her. I much prefer our harmony, to fuck her in earnest and without the tension that comes with complicated games. I know adapting hasn't been easy for her, but I'm trying to make up for it by giving her everything I can. The more effort she makes for me, the more I give back in return. Of all the lessons I've taught her, this is maybe the most important one. It's the answer to both of our peace and happiness, for as long as I can taste her pussy and drink in her existence, I'm as happy as I'll ever be.

"The usual," I say, accepting the drink.

She reaches up to undo my tie. I enjoy the pressure of her slight weight where her body rests against mine. I love the sight of her beautiful face. I fucking revel in knowing she's mine. I get hard knowing I'm going to bend her over the sofa and fuck her before letting her work on her sewing machine in the spare room I've converted into a working space. I don't like the long hours she puts in, but she doesn't sleep more than a few hours anyway, hasn't since the night of the shooting. Working is better than staring at the ceiling with an idle mind. Idle minds are unhealthy. They reflect too much.

I trace the V-neck of her blouse. It's a frilly affair with soft layers. "Did you make this?"

"Yes."

She makes a lot of her clothes now. I like how she dresses. Her garments are feminine and soft, reminding me of sweet smelling roses and gentle daisies.

"It's nice," I say.

"Thank you," she whispers.

Taking a sip of the drink, I bend down and press our mouths together. When she parts her lips, I feed her the alcohol. I let her swallow before using my tongue to taste the whiskey on hers. I lap at her mouth like I'm planning on eating her out later, giving her a preview of what I have in mind for her pussy.

She moans. *Fuck.* It's all it takes. I catch fire. Putting the drink aside, I reach for the buttons of her blouse. The silk is smooth under my fingers, but it's nothing compared to her skin.

"Maxime." She pushes with her palms on my chest and bend backwards to escape my kiss. "I want to ask you something."

I chase after her mouth, catching her around the waist as I lower her onto the couch. "I know."

"Wait." She bites her lip, staring up at me with her big, irresistible eyes. "I don't want you to think I'm fucking you so you'd say yes."

I push my hand under her skirt and trail my fingers up the inside of her leg. So warm. So soft. I barely contain my excitement as I move higher. I'm like an eager teenager on his first date. My hand trembles when I finally cup the juncture of her legs. *Double fuck.*

"How can I deny you anything when you're wet like this?" I groan against her lips, grinding my erection against her sex.

"Maxime." She gives me a little frown. Adorable. "I'm serious."

"So am I." Catching the elastic of her panties, I work them down her thighs. I leave them on her knees and bunch her skirt up to her waist. I use one hand to unzip my fly and take out my cock while keeping my weight on the other that rests next to her face. Her long, silky hair brushes against my fingers.

"I don't want Benoit to drive me," she says. "He hates babysitting me."

I shudder as the head of my cock pushes against her slick pussy lips. "He does what I tell him to do." Pleasure rips from my balls up my spine as I sink deep.

She gasps, threading her fingers through my hair. "I want to drive myself."

Goddamn. Fuck. She feels good. "Why?"

"I haven't driven a car since I got my driver's license in South Africa." She whimpers when I start moving. "I want to be independent."

"Fine." I'm not going to last.

"Really?" She pulls on my hair, bringing our mouths close. "You mean it?"

"After you've practiced driving on the right-hand side."

Her expression softens with pleasure and gratitude.

"Benoit and my men follow wherever you go."

She locks her legs around my waist, lifting her pelvis to take more. "Okay."

"Fuck, Zoe."

That obedience. The easy agreement. Letting me have my way. I break. I fuck her like a madman and come even before I've tasted her or bent her over the armrest like I've fantasized, before I've taken care of her pleasure.

Resting my forehead against hers, I try to get my erratic heartbeat under control. "Now look what you've done."

She smiles. It's not just another smile, but one she smiles for *me*. It's a selfless one that takes my breath away.

"I didn't make you come, you naughty girl."

"I don't mind," she whispers, stretching lazily. "It was good, anyway."

"It wasn't good. It was fucking great, and it's far from over."

She stares at me with sated eyes—trusting eyes—as I push a hand between our bodies and find her clit. She lets me take care of her with her body stuffed full of my cock and cum. It doesn't take long before I recognize the signs. Her pupils dilate and her gaze turns hazy. Rosy pink colors her cheeks. Her inner muscles clench, and her head falls back as she says my name.

The top button of her blouse is undone, a job I abandoned in my haste to get into her panties. I try to finish that intention now, fumbling with the second button. Fuck it. I tear the blouse open in another fit of haste. Her chest heaves with labored breaths as I roll a thumb over her clit, working her fast to bring her up to speed with me. I brush the fabric of her blouse aside and leave her breasts covered in lace. Like this, she looks ravished. Devoured. Undone. Just looking at her makes my cock grow hard again. I swell inside her, stretching her inner muscles.

"Maxime," she moans, every kind of emotion coloring her voice.

"Say it again," I demand with a growl against her ear. I want to hear more of that rainbow, of that complex spectrum of feelings. It fuels me to move harder, to make her shout it.

"I love you," she cries out.

Everything inside me simultaneously combusts and freezes. I fill her up with release even as my body goes as rigid as a rod. I'm ecstatic and devastated. I'm roaring in victory and hurting with something I can't name. For the first time in my life, Delphine's diagnosis is a heavy burden on my shoulders. Pretty little innocent flowers turn their faces to the sun, not to monsters like me. The only reward I can offer is sinking as deep as her body can take me and pounding my ownership into her with a too-harsh rhythm.

Struggling for breath, I push up on my elbows to frame her face between my palms. Tears leak from the corners of her eyes. I kiss them away, offering my lips in exchange for my lack of words.

My thrusts turn even more grueling. I can come ten times more like this. Pleasure already builds again at the base of my spine, but I slow my pace to time our releases. When we finally come, it's a powerful eruption of intertwined relief.

I fucking fly.

She falls.

All I can give is catching her.

CHAPTER 16

Zoe

I wake up to the first glorious day after another freezing winter and realize this ocean has been my view for the past eighteen months. Eighteen months of giving myself to Maxime. The realization jars me. I stare at my face in the mirror, the make-up brush frozen in my hand. I'm trying. I really am. I can't say he's not treating me well. After I dropped the bomb about loving him, nothing has changed for the better, but at least nothing has changed for the worst, either. We're maintaining our status quo.

Maxime steps from the dressing room wearing a white shirt and blue suit tailored to the latest fashion, paired with Italian shoes. He looks smart and impossibly handsome. He's focused on fitting a cufflink, but when he catches my gaze, he walks up behind me and places his hands on my shoulders. Our eyes remained locked for a moment before he swoops down and places a kiss on my neck.

"Good morning, *cherie*." His gray eyes turn a shade warmer. "You look beautiful."

"Thank you." With the restriction in my throat, the words sound thick.

He frowns. "What's wrong?"

"Nothing." I force a smile. "I'm running late, that's all."

The lie comes with effort. He knows me well enough by now not to buy it. Besides, I'm always early.

Kneading my shoulders, he says, "Try again."

He won't give up until I tell him. Biting my lip, I gauge his mood. "I've just realized it's been eighteen months."

Some of the warmth in his gaze dissipates. "We should go out and celebrate."

It's hardly something I want to celebrate, but I know better than to fail this test. "Whenever you want."

He brushes my hair over my shoulder. "I meant to speak to you about tonight."

The way he hesitates makes me tense. "What about tonight?"

"We have to attend a gallery opening." Searching my face, he adds, "With my family."

"Your *whole* family?"

"Everyone, including Alexis. I wouldn't expose you to them if I didn't have to, but this is an important event. We have a lot invested in the gallery."

"I could stay at home?" I offer hopefully.

"No." His tone is curt. "Hiding you at home would send the wrong message."

"Which is?"

"That I don't respect you."

"Oh." His respect never crossed my mind. "Do you?"

"Of course." He twists a strand of hair around his finger. "I admire you."

"If people think you don't respect me, how would that be a problem?"

"People you don't respect are expendable."

Goosebumps break out over my arms. "I see." No one has tried to kill me since the drive-by shooting, but the threat is never out of my thoughts for long.

"All right." My smile is shaky. I don't like Maxime's family. I definitely don't look forward to seeing them at a gala event, which will be stressful enough as it is.

He squeezes my shoulders. "Sylvie will be there."

At least there's something to look forward to.

Gripping my chin, he turns my face to the side and kisses my lips. "I'll see you tonight. Be ready at seven."

I hurry through the rest of my grooming and go down to the kitchen to prepare my latest breakfast craze—a spirulina and berry smoothie.

Francine regards me from where she's rolling out dough for a quiche. She's long since given up on setting out my breakfast, but she still dumps the granulated sugar in the trashcan and replaces it with cubes. In turn, I buy sticky brown sugar and fill up the pot I bought. It's a childish circle of spitefulness, but neither of us is prepared to surrender.

"You better start wearing sunblock," she says, studying me from under her lashes. "You're getting more freckles."

Twisting the lid onto my portable cup, I smile. "Maxime loves my freckles."

She laughs. "Any man who says he likes freckles is a liar."

"I'll let Maxime know," I say on my way to the door.

"That he's a liar? Oh, trust me, he knows, but so do you."

I turn on my heel. "Maybe you should tell him that to his face."

"He knows how I feel. He promised me things when we were together." Leaning her hands on the counter, she returns my fake smile. "What did he promise *you*?"

"What happens between Maxime and me doesn't concern you."

I leave without saying goodbye, holding my head high as I walk through the door, but her words have thorns, and they hook into my heart. I can't get them out of my head during the drive to school or for the duration of my classes.

. . .

My brain feels mushy from a whole day of complicated pattern calculations and mulling over what Francine has said. When I get home by six, I have a headache. The stress of anticipating tonight doesn't help. I take a painkiller and am ready at the hour Maxime has stipulated. At seven sharp, he enters the bedroom with a bouquet of pink roses.

"For the most beautiful woman in the world," he says, offering them to me.

"They're gorgeous." I inhale their scent. "Thank you."

"You're welcome." He runs his gaze over my dress. "One of your designs?"

"Yes." It's a black halter neck with a short train at the back. The skirt is decorated with a few black feathers. They add texture and a focal point to the otherwise simple cut.

"Absolutely stunning." He cups my hips. "Even more so on this body."

I've grown accustomed to his compliments. Maxime isn't someone to offer empty appraisal. He means what he says. I can't help but wonder what compliments he whispered into Francine's ear. For her to be so bitter over their breakup, it had to have been serious.

"Maxime." I put the flowers on the bed, weighing my words. "How committed were things between Francine and you?"

He studies me for a moment. "I told you. It was sex."

"Like us? We're sex, too. Nothing more, right?"

His expression darkens. "There's no comparison between you and Francine."

"What's the difference?"

His fingers tighten on my flesh. "You're a keeper."

"What did you promise her?"

"Nothing." His look is chastising. "I don't make promises I can't keep."

"That's not how she sees it."

He sets me aside and drops his arms by his side. "What did she say to you?"

"That you promised her *things*."

He chuckles. "Believe me, if I promised her *things*, you wouldn't be here."

I'd be with Alexis, and she would've shared Maxime's bed. Yet here I am. "Why?"

"Why what?" He checks his watch. "We don't have time for this, Zoe."

"Why me? Why not Francine or someone else? Is it just because of the diamonds?" I ask, although, I find that hard to believe. He didn't have to keep me forever. He could've let me go when his deal was secured. Maybe he's worried Damian will reverse his decision if he finds out the truth, if this crazy scheme Maxime mentioned ever works out.

A nerve ticks under his eye. "I know what you're asking, Zoe."

"I'm asking why you chose *me* as your property."

"No." He grips my chin. "You're asking if I feel differently about you than other women. The answer is yes. I've never cared more, but you're also asking if I love you. The answer to that, as much as it saddens me, is and will always be no."

His words drive into my heart. They twist and hurt. I lay a palm over the ache, willing it to stop, but I can't turn my feelings off. I can only suffer them knowing there will never be a remedy. Why did I have to scratch the scab off? We were doing so well.

"Maybe…" A suppressed sob turns into a soft gasp. "Maybe you feel more than you realize."

"I *know*."

"How?" I exclaim. "The way you behave—"

"Is designed to make you happy. Love is selfless, like you. Me, I'm the opposite of everything you are. I'm selfish."

Stupidly, I cling to hope. "You're being very hard on yourself."

"No, Zoe." His eyes are solemn. "If I loved you, I would've set you free."

What he says rings true. Yet I don't want it to be. It's too agonizing to bear. I press my free hand over my stomach to where the ache spreads, holding in the raw emotions that threaten to tumble out.

"I wish to God I was capable of love," he says. "I want to give it to you more than I want to do anything in the world, but this is who I am." He strokes a thumb over my chin. "I can't change my nature."

His words are killing me. Between Francine and me, she's the one who's better off. At least she doesn't have to live with him day and night while suffering the knowledge for an unloving eternity. I'm so fucking pathetic. Why do I do this to myself over and over? Why do I keep wanting us to be different?

"If you can't love me," I say, "set me free." It hurts too much to live like this. "Please, Maxime. We can just forget about everything. I won't lay charges. I won't tell a soul. Not even Damian. I promise."

"You know I can't do that."

"Why not?" I cry out.

"Because I can't live without you."

I can only stare at him, trying to get a grip on the old hurt that won't let go. Just when I think I've accepted my situation, I have to go and lift the lid on the pot of my twisted emotions.

"I'm sorry." Folding his arms around me, he pulls me close. "If it makes you feel better, I'm living to make it up to you."

It doesn't, but there's nothing to be done about it. It's not going to change, and I'm not going to cry about it.

My heart must be hardening slowly but surely, because my eyes are dry when I pull away. "Thank you for being honest with me." I'm bleeding inside, but I put on a smile. I've learned from the master.

He kisses my lips. The action is tender, apologetic. It's like a kiss on a child's cut knee. His eyes fold in the corners. Giving me a thoughtful nod like he's just ticked a task off his to-do list, he takes the flowers and walks to the bathroom. I act on autopilot, dumping lipstick and perfume into my clutch bag. Anything to keep my hands busy and hide how I'm feeling.

When he returns, he takes my hand like his words haven't torn me apart. "Shall we go?"

I know the right answer. "Yes."

"Good." He kisses my cheek. "I think you'll like the exhibition."

We drive to town without making conversation. He takes a few calls, but, like always, avoids discussing *business* in front of me. For my own protection, I assume.

The minute we enter the gallery, guests swamp Maxime. To be honest, I'm happy for the reprieve. I need some space from him.

When he hands me a glass of champagne that he takes from a passing waiter, I say, "I'm going to look for Sylvie."

He nods, casts a glance around the room, and flicks his fingers at Benoit.

The place is packed. Making my way through the masses with Benoit following closely, I pass contemporary paintings featuring garbage. Rotting food, one-eyed dolls, and burnt flowers are the subjects. I get the message, but Maxime was wrong. I hate it.

The crowd thins toward the back. A room leads off to the right. I go inside. A mobile light display illuminates nails in the wall. Mumbling, "Excuse me," I push through the spectators who entered behind me and make my way to the room on the opposite side. Just before I reach the archway, Sylvie's bubbly laugh reaches my ears. Oh, thank God. I'm not going to dump my problems on her, but I can do with a friend. I'm about to enter when my name pops up in her conversation. I stop in my tracks.

"I don't know how you can stand her," a female voice says. "Her clothes are so distasteful."

"The princess stuff is the worst," Sylvie says.

"Did you see her dress when they walked in tonight?"

"Hideous."

"Someone should tell her."

"Ha," Sylvie says. "I just can't be bothered."

Sucking in a breath, I lean a hand on the wall. My heart starts thumping with a heavy beat. It's a beat I recognize well, one that pumps with the knowledge of betrayal.

"I hate how naïve she is," Sylvie continues.

They can't be talking about me. Sylvie is my friend.

"I don't see what Maxime sees in her," the other woman says.

"Boobs and ass, obviously," Sylvie replies. "The fact that he won't marry her says a lot."

A wave of heat rises from my stomach to my chest, making me feel sick.

A hand lands on my arm. "Are you all right?"

I look from the hand to its owner. Benoit. "Fine." I down the champagne and hand him the glass. "I need another drink."

Turning around, I go in the opposite direction. I don't stop until I'm somewhere in the middle of the floor, hidden by strangers. Benoit hands me another glass. I thank him and swallow it down.

"Hey," he says, "you better go easy on the booze."

I hand him the empty glass. He's right. I'm not my father, but maybe I am the naïve princess Sylvie described. I fell for her deceit, didn't I? I was stupid enough to believe she was sincere. Taking a glass of juice from a nearby cocktail table, I keep an eye on the archway.

Not long after, Sylvie and Noelle exit. They walk to a small group, smiling as they near. Raphael, Cecile, Emile, Hadrienne, and Alexis are standing together.

"Are those girls being bitches to you?" Benoit asks, following my gaze.

"No."

"I wouldn't worry about their opinion."

I look at him, really look at him for the first time. After he's asked me to keep my distance, I've respected his request. We never drive together any longer, but I've noticed him hastily shoving pastries down his throat in his car before following me to class.

"Do you eat croissants for breakfast every day?" I ask.

His face scrunches up. "What?"

"That can't be healthy or good for your weight."

He drags a hand over his stomach. "The girls aren't complaining."

"From now on, I'll make you a smoothie."

"A fucking what?"

"If you follow me, I may as well watch out for you."

"I'm not following you. I'm protecting you. *I'm* the one watching out for *you*."

I'm hurting inside, my chest throbbing like an open wound, but the banter is like a Band-Aid on a cut. Maybe it's just a really good distraction.

"Well," I smile, "all of that is about to change."

"Here we go." He rolls his eyes. "Now I'm your pet project."

"Nothing like that," I say, swatting him on the arm. "But you're done pushing me away."

"Listen here, lady. I missed five football matches because I'm trailing after you."

"Then maybe we should eat lunch in a brasserie where you can catch up on your matches. Two birds with one stone."

"Getting friendly with the staff?" a voice cuts in.

I turn. Alexis stands in front of me, dressed in a tux. My stomach roils. Vivid images of the woman he tortured run through my mind.

"It's been too long," he drawls.

"Not long enough," I mutter.

He chuckles. "A sense of humor, too. No wonder my brother is so taken with you."

I glance at where I left Maxime. He's talking to his father. Maxime's expression is dark and his gaze narrow as he regards Raphael from under his eyelashes. Raphael moves closer, saying something in Maxime's ear. Maxime's hand balls into a fist at his side.

"Speaking of which, how is my brother treating you?" Alexis asks.

"That's none of your business." I look over his shoulder. Benoit has moved a short distance away, discreetly giving us space, but he's still within earshot.

"I was just going to say you're always welcome at my place if you need saving."

"I don't think Maxime will appreciate you talking like that."

"You were supposed to be mine," he says with a wink. "It's only natural that I watch out for you."

"Like you did for that poor woman we found in your apartment?"

His smile is practiced. Underneath the gesture runs malice. "What woman?"

"I'll never pretend it didn't happen," I say, lowering my voice.

"Calm down, Zoe. You think you know everything, don't you?"

"I know enough."

Laughing, he tips back his glass. "You have no idea."

This evening has gotten too much. "Benoit, I'd like to go home."

"Running?" Alexis asks. "Do I scare you, little Zoe?"

A strong hand closes around my upper arm. I look up into Maxime's thunderous face.

"I told you to stay away from her," Maxime says in a cold tone, slipping an arm around my waist and pulling me against his side.

"I can hardly avoid her at a social gathering." Alexis's gaze moves to his family. "Although, it seems everyone else is."

A muscle ticks at Maxime's temple. "If you want a fight, say so. Don't pick one. I'm happy to take it outside."

Alexis lifts his hands. "I come in peace."

"Is that why you went behind my back again?"

"Father invited me to the club for lunch. The opportunity came up. It would've been foolish to waste it. If you'd been there more often like you're supposed to be, you wouldn't have to accuse me of stealing your fifteen minutes of fame." He trails his gaze over me. "We all know where you prefer to spend your evenings."

Sylvie's voice rings over the noise of the crowd. "Zoe!" She makes her way over and takes my hands. "Where have you been? I've been looking all over for you. Look at you. What a beautiful dress. Did you make it?"

I pull away.

"Has Alexis been keeping you busy?" She pouts at her cousin. "Are you bothering my friend?"

"Just leaving," he says, bowing in my direction.

"You do that," Maxime grits out.

"What's going on?" Sylvie asks when Alexis walks off.

"Nothing new," Maxime says. His eyes remain fixed on his brother's back as Alexis walks to the bar and orders a drink.

"I'm in town until Saturday," Sylvie says. "Shall we grab some pizza? Girls' night. You won't mind, will you, Max?"

"Actually," I say, "I have exams coming up."

"What about the weekend after?"

"I'll be putting all my time into my second level proposal."

She makes a face. "That's too bad. Promise you'll call me?"

I barely manage a smile.

"Ready to go?" Maxime asks.

It's hard to hide my relief. "Please."

He studies my face with a piercing gaze. "Everything all right?"

"I'd just like to go. I'm really tired."

He bends down to kiss the shell of my ear. "Bear with me for another few minutes."

Taking my hand, he leads me to his family. The closer we get, the tighter my insides twist. Cecile looks up. The smile vanishes from her face when she sees me. Hadrienne's expression grows hostile.

"Goodnight, Maman." Maxime kisses her cheeks. "Hadrienne." He barely looks at his father.

I do the forced round of kisses, bidding everyone goodnight like Maxime expects of me. Maxime's family returns the polite greeting, putting up their side of the show while Noelle only stands there with a smirk.

It's only in the car that I breathe again. Sinking back into the cool leather of the seat, I wind down the window and drag a hand over my brow.

"What the fuck is going on, Zoe? And, don't tell me it's nothing."

Taking a deep breath, I blow it out slowly. "Did you ask Sylvie to be my friend?"

Maxime looks at me. "Why do you ask that?"

"Just answer the question."

He taps a thumb on the wheel, seeming to consider the answer. After a moment, he says, "She owed me a favor."

His admission tramples on the heart he's already ripped from my chest. "What exactly did you ask her to do?"

"I asked her to give you her number."

"On that Sunday we met?" I exclaim.

"Yes." He shrugs. "I had to cover for her to go out with a group of friends. She told her father she was visiting me." He repeats, "She owed me."

As if that makes it okay. My spirits sink even lower. "The day I told you I wanted to have coffee with her, did you order her to go with me?"

"I called her and told her to expect a call from you. I suggested taking you to a brasserie where you'd be safe."

My breath catches at the implication. "Did you ask her to talk me into giving you a chance?"

"I told her to try and convince you, yes, but only for your own good."

"How's lying to me and pretending to be my friend for my own good?"

"Accepting your situation is for your own good. I want you to be happy, Zoe. Is that so bad?"

"Don't you realize how wrong what you've done is? Are you even sorry?"

"No." His tone is flat. "I'm not sorry for taking care of your emotional comfort."

"God, Maxime." Gripping my head in my hands, I groan in frustration. "You can't keep on doing this."

He shoots me a sidelong glance. "Doing what?"

"Betraying me. You've pushed me as far as I can go, do you hear me? You've pushed me to my limits, and God help me—" I cut off before I threaten the man who owns my life.

His voice turns hard. "God help you with what, Zoe?"

I sag back. "I'm afraid of what I'll do the day you push me over."

"Nothing," he says with blind conviction. "You'll do nothing, because I'll always be there to catch you."

"Please, Maxime." I sag a little lower. "Please stop manipulating me. Why can't you simply be honest?"

He pulls off on the side of the road and brings the car to a jerky halt. "You want honest?"

"Yes!" I'm tired. Depleted. Empty. I have nothing left to give. "Yes, damn you."

"Get out of the car."

My hand clenches on the door handle. "Maxime."

"Now isn't a time to test me."

I open the door and get out, stumbling in the tall grass with my heels. Before I'm a step away from the car, Maxime is there, his strong arms wrapping around my waist. He pushes me forward, bending my body over the hood. Our shadows fall tall over the road in the headlights, two bodies merged as one. The stark silhouette is a lie. The truth is the invisible picture of our estranged souls.

Flipping my skirt up, he rips off my underwear and pushes a knee between my legs. His zipper makes a tearing sound. His cock is at my entrance before I have time to gasp.

"You want the truth?" he breathes against my ear. "This is the truth."

With one, hard thrust, he buries himself so deep inside me his groin slams against my ass. My body shifts over the warm metal of his car. Grabbing a fistful of my hair, he holds me in place and gives me more truth. My inner muscles tighten around him.

"Show me," he says as he gives me the kind of rough that makes my toes curl.

It's no different than pushing me down and making me kneel. My body's reaction is my bitter truth and his sweet victory. I try to deny it. I fight the pleasure that winds around my insides. I fight the lie of the picture on the ground, but he refuses to let me hide. He folds an arm around my body and pushes the heel of his palm on my clit. The harder I fight, the harder he fucks me. There's no way but down. Falling. There's no way out other than surrendering.

I come with a cry and a shudder, every muscle locking in pleasure, but I take no joy from it. I keep still, letting him use me until he finds his release.

"Fuck. What you do to me..." he says, caressing my hip. "Goddamn, Zoe."

Turning my face to the side, I rest my cheek on the metal and stare with non-seeing eyes at the dark ocean. Just like that, the rebellion is over. He squashed it even before it has started.

He wins. Again.

CHAPTER 17

One year later

Maxime

The wind rips through Zoe's long hair when I steer the boat from the jetty of our family holiday home in Corsica. The place is isolated, a pretty piece of paradise. The stretch of beach is private, meaning I can fuck her wherever and whenever I like without worrying about spectators. This weekend is ours alone. No guards. No business.

She takes an elastic band from her wrist and binds the long tresses in a high ponytail. Then she shimmies out of her bikini bottoms and unties the top. The triangles fall away from her breasts. They jiggle when she climbs down the steps and stretches out on the front of the boat. I battle to tear my gaze from her naked body, only managing when I have to navigate through the dangerous rocks close to the cliffs.

I steer the boat to the small island not far off and anchor in the deeper water so we don't get washed up with low tide. After yanking off my shirt, I adjust my hard-on and grab two glasses of champagne and a bowl of strawberries from the table under the awning. Armed with my weapons, I make my way over to where she's tanning with her gorgeous breasts and pussy exposed to the sun.

She pushes up onto her arms when my shadow falls over her.

I hand her a glass. "Here you go, *cherie*."

Squinting up at me, she smiles. Fuck. That smile. If my life should end now, I'll die a happy man.

I stretch out on my side next to her, propping myself up on an elbow. "Congratulations, little flower." I clink my glass to hers. "I'm proud of you."

A shadow creeps over her smile. I know what's going through her mind.

"You deserved to pass," I say. "You did great."

"Did I?"

Unable to resist, I brush my knuckles over a nipple. "You worked hard."

"Hard work isn't always enough."

Taking a mouthful of champagne, I close my lips around the warm tip of her breast, bathing it in the fizzy liquid.

She gasps. "It's cold."

Letting the champagne dribble over her breast, I set the glass aside to test between her thighs. "Always wet for me." Her reaction pleases me to no end.

"Maxime," she chastises as I roll over her, making the champagne slosh over the rim of her glass onto her stomach.

I lap up the spillage. "Delicious."

"You're impossible," she says with a laugh.

"Happy." I mean it. I can't think of a time I felt happier. I carefully push a finger into her tight heat. "Are you?"

"Yes," she says on a sigh, throwing her head back.

"Show me." I watch her greedily as I move my finger.

Her pupils dilate, and her blue eyes turn hazy. A soft moan falls from her lips. Leaving her glass on the side, she reaches for the elastic of my swimming trunks and pushes them over my hips. My cock jumps free, hard and aching. Always ready.

Freeing the finger I teased her with, I slide it past her lips. She curls her tongue around the tip, making my over-eager cock twitch. When I pull out, she bites down gently. My skin comes alive. Every cell in my body starts to hum. The scar tissue on my chest tingles. I catch her nape and bring her lips closer to mine as I drag a flattened palm down her belly to her sex. I claim her mouth as I rub my thumb over her clit. She goes soft in my hold, surrendering her control. I take it with the same abandonment that I took her life, tangling our tongues while I grab the root of my cock and rub the pre-cum over her clit.

"Maxime."

The way she says my name makes me lose it. I was going to take it slow, but I slide all the way in until I hit a barrier and her back arches.

"Good?" I ask, breaking the kiss.

"Mm."

"Show me."

I fuck her in all earnest. Everything will never be enough. I can't explain it. I can't put a label on or words to it. I only know she makes me want more. She wraps her legs around my ass and slams back when I thrust. Our dance is well choreographed and perfectly timed. We're breathing in tune. She never asked me to love her again, but the words hang in the air. It's in the way she rolls her hips and pants as we pick up our pace. It's in the way she holds my eyes and lets me see the desperate need burning out of control.

"You're mine," I say into our kiss, pounding harder into her.

She takes the roughness and gives it back with good measure, her nails digging into my shoulders as she pushes on them to flip us around. For her, I roll over. The way she rides me with her head thrown back and her breasts pushed out is enough to shatter what's left of my control.

I lock my hands around her waist. "Come with me."

She cries out when I roll my hips and hit that spot that makes her reach her *petite mort* quicker.

"Tell me, *cherie*." I lean forward to steal a kiss. "Tell me how it is."

"You know how it is."

Pleasure coils, ready to erupt. "Tell me, anyway."

"Perfect," she whispers.

I explode, my body contracting as every physical sensation I'm capable of aligns in my dick. An answering shudder runs through her body. Her inner muscles clench on my cock, milking me dry.

Taking her face between my hands, I kiss her. I don't know for how long our bodies are fused like this, our mouths and hips joined, but the shadows are longer when I finally convince myself to pull out.

She lays on top of me in a beautiful disarray of dark hair and damp skin, her breasts pushed flat against my chest.

"Perfect," I agree. "I can stay like this forever."

"Then let's," she says, splaying a palm over the ugly skin that covers my breastbone.

Joy infinitely more powerful than the climax still reverberating in my lower body bursts through my chest. It catches me off-guard, shocking me into silence. It's unlike anything I've felt. Gripping her fingers, I hold her hand over my heart.

"Yes," I say. "Let's."

She snuggles with a content little sigh, burying her nose in my neck.

Like I said, "Perfect."

ON SUNDAY, our forever comes to an end, but the perfect lingers when I hold her hand as we board the ferry. The minute we step into my house near Cassis, my father calls and summons me for dinner. When I kiss her and tell her I won't be home late, the only remainder of the paradise we shared is her tan.

We've fallen into an easy rhythm, Zoe and I. She's adapted. All is good. I *feel* good. My mood sours, though, when I walk through the door of my parents' house and find Alexis in the foyer with a glass of wine in his hand.

"Brother." He gives me a cool smile. "I didn't know you were coming."

He'll never forgive me for the lesson I taught him. Together with his envy of my first-born status, it'll be a rift between us for the rest of our days. Not that I care. It's not as if there were ever any brotherly feelings between us before.

I hand my coat to the housekeeper. "Is that a problem?"

Alexis smiles at the young woman. She's new. They never last long with my mother. "I'm just surprised you were able to tear yourself away from Zoe."

"There you are," Maman says, exiting the kitchen. "Come on, Max. Help me carve the lamb."

Throwing a taunting smile over my shoulder at Alexis, I follow my mother to the kitchen.

She pats my cheek. "It's good to have both my boys at home for dinner. That old table is too big for just your father and me." She smiles. "But soon, it will be filled with grandchildren."

Ah. That explains her happy disposition. Me, I'm apathetic about it. It's a duty, like the business. "Don't start, Maman."

"Oh, no. You're not going to deny me that pleasure."

I take the carving knife from the wooden block on the counter. "Don't expect anything too soon."

She pours gravy into a serving bowl. "You're not getting any younger."

For a moment, I think about children. I think about a boy who'll follow in my footsteps, and a girl who'll inherit Maman's fate. I won't say I'm unhappy with my life, but I'm suddenly not sure if the family future is a gift or curse. Before Zoe, I wouldn't have even posed the question, but she has a way of making me look at things through her eyes, seeing them differently.

"Don't you want children?" Maman asks with big eyes.

"Of course, I do."

She dries her hands on her apron, her posture relaxing visibly.

"Good. The honeymoon is over. It's time to focus on family and making babies, but you shouldn't forget the business. You've been neglecting it, allowing Alexis to fill your shoes. Your place is at the head of the family, Max. Don't let worldly distractions make you forget that." She points a finger at me. "You're the one who's supposed to take over your father's business. Alexis can't run it like you can."

I arrange a slice of meat on the serving platter. "You're not telling me anything I don't already know."

"I have news you don't already know," my father says from the door. He tilts his head toward the hallway. "Join me."

Maman throws her hands in the air. "Seriously, Raphael? We're about to sit down for dinner."

"The lamb is already dead," he says. "It's not going anywhere."

Maman switches on the warming drawer with a scoff. "Make it quick. I've slaved over this meal all day."

My father kisses her cheek when she scurries past him. "You're the one who said Max should pay more attention to the business."

"Were you eavesdropping on our conversation?" Maman asks with a teasing smile.

My father kisses her again, this time on the lips.

She shoos him away.

Alexis leans against a wall when we exit, sipping his wine. He watches me from over the rim of his glass, his gaze following my progress as I follow my father to his study.

"What's up?" I ask when I've closed the door.

Father shoves his hands into his pockets. "Damian Hart is out."

My mind jolts into action, considering the implications. "Since when?"

"This morning. I've just heard from Zane."

Hence the last-minute call to come over for dinner. "Is your informant still on the inside?"

"He got out a week ago."

"That's a coincidence."

"He bribed the parole committee."

"Let me guess. You provided the bribe money."

"Of course." My father walks to the wet bar. "We need to keep tabs on Hart now more than ever. Da Costa is just the man to do it."

"If Hart doesn't play into our hands, I'll have to pay him a visit."

"With his sister." He lifts the carafe. "Scotch?"

"Thanks." I tense when I think about putting Zoe in such a position. What incentive does she have not to tell Damian the truth now that she knows I won't kill her brother? "The fact that she's living in France as my mistress should be enough to convince Hart to keep the business relations good between us."

"She's a means to an end, son. Don't forget that." He pours a stiff shot of Scotch and hands me a glass. "We'll use her as we must, any way we have to."

I don't fucking think so. Zoe is my responsibility. I own her, body and soul. I'll decide what's best for her and how her future will evolve, not my father or anyone else.

My father brings his drink to his lips. "I want Alexis in on the deal."

My fingers clench around the glass. "What deal?"

"The diamonds. I want you to teach him the ropes."

Suspicion goes off like an alarm bell in my mind. "Why?"

"You'll have your hands tied up with the business here when you take over in a few months."

When I honor the deal my father has made, he can finally retire. "The deal with Dalton is the crux of our business. Everything depends on that deal. Alexis can work with the Italians and run the docks."

"No." My father slams his glass down on the desk. "The Italians are your responsibility. Trying to escape it will give them the wrong idea."

"I'm not trying to escape it. I'm just saying Alexis is in a better position to deal with the taxes."

"Leaving you free to deal with Hart or to make sure no one else gets close to his sister?"

"What about you?" I close the step between us. "What's your agenda? Making sure Alexis gets in on the big deals while pawning me off to the Italians?"

He waves a finger at my face. "Watch your tone."

"I don't even know why we're having this discussion. In a few months' time, I'll be calling the shots, deciding how Alexis is involved."

My father's face turns red. "*If* you honor the contract."

I narrow my eyes with a smile. "Are you hoping I won't?"

"Don't put words in my mouth."

"Then don't give me reason to." I leave the glass on his desk and turn for the door. "Maman is waiting. Shall we have dinner?"

When I walk through that door, the power has shifted. I'm holding it all in my fist. Everything. I let the knowledge sink in, soothing my deepest concern—keeping Zoe safe.

CHAPTER 18

Zoe

The shorter and colder the days grow, the harder I work. By December, I'm only sleeping four hours a night. The closer I get to the year-end fashion show, the more my anxiety climbs. Only four of the girls who are left will continue to the final level. Our designs will be judged by an independent panel, and no one, not even Madame Page or Maxime, can determine the outcome.

I want to do well. I want to win Madame Page's approval and show I've earned my place, which is why I put in more effort and hours than anyone in the class. I stitch faster than Thérèse and make fewer mistakes than Miss Page's favorite student, Christine. I always hand in my homework early. I do research at home, and I visit fashion exhibitions and museums with Maxime on the weekends. I pour my heart into my collection. When the day of the fashion show arrives, I'm positive I'll have good results. I'll go as far as to say I'm hopeful of swaying Madame Page.

Maxime takes me early to the performing arts theatre where the event is held so I can add the finishing touches to my garments.

He carries my needlework case to the garderobe where our collections are already stored and leaves it on the worktable to wrap his arms around me.

"You'll do great." His eyes warm with a smile. "I'm proud of you."

"Thank you." I pull away and flip open the lid of my case. The model who'll be modeling my wedding dress has lost weight after a recent bout of gastro, and I have to take in the waist. There's not enough time to remake the bodice, but I can take in a few centimeters on the sides by hand.

"Hey." Maxime catches my wrist.

My cheeks grow hot at the heated look in his eyes.

"Haven't you forgotten something?" he asks in a husky voice.

That voice is enough to make me forget about everything. "I'm sorry." I go on tiptoes to kiss his lips. "I'm a little distracted."

He cups my nape. "I know." Pulling me close, he kisses me in the way that makes every follicle come alive. Lethargic heat flushes my body, making me wet. I throb and ache for him. Just before my knees give out, he breaks the kiss.

My whole being mourns the loss of his touch and warmth. We stare into each other's eyes, wordless understanding passing between us. I'm his. He's mine. Our give and take isn't equal, but there's comfort in knowing we belong to each other and that we've somehow managed to make our warped situation work.

"Good luck," he mouths.

"No." I press my hand over his mouth. "Don't say it. It's bad luck."

Folding his fingers around my wrist, he kisses my palm before moving my hand away. "If I don't let you go now…"

He doesn't have to finish the sentence. We both know we'll end up in a dark corner fucking against a wall if he doesn't leave. How did we get to this point? How did I get so addicted to him? When did he become so handsome and dear to me?

"Break a leg," he says with a wicked smile, turning on his heel and leaving me in a puddle of desire.

I give myself a little shake to break the trance. A tinge of fear slips into my elation. I know exactly why he makes me lose track of everything, even here and now at this critical event. It's because he overshadows everything. He's grown more important than anything else in my life, even more important than my studies and my dream to be a designer. Somewhere in the knotted threads of our unconventional relationship, *he* became my dream.

The realization startles me. It frightens me. Whatever power I've given Maxime over me in the past is nothing compared to this. This is atomic. This can destroy me.

Voices coming from the hallway pull me back to the present. A few classmates file through the door, chatting animatedly. We're all on edge about tonight, over-excited and anxious.

I thread a needle and set to work. My fingertips are already pricked raw. The grand finale, my wedding dress, is my dream design. I've poured everything I am and ever wanted to be into the dress. It's whimsical, romantic, and feminine. It has a sweetheart bodice and a meringue skirt layered with diamante studded net fabric. The color is the softest of pinks, a barely visible hue that bleeds out from the virginal white at the top to the darker hem of the skirt.

After a couple of hours of careful adjustments, my back is aching. Stepping away from the dress form, I study my work. My chest swells. A feeling of peace dawns on me even as my breath quickens. It's a warm feeling, but it's nothing like the arousal Maxime elicits. This is pride. This is my best. I put a hand over my heart. I *love* this dress. I love it for everything it represents, but it's more than pride and love. There's something else underneath the layers, something that causes these reactions of glowing contentedness and combustible love inside me. It's imagining wearing it for Maxime. It's imagining him in a dark suit under the angelic lights of a stained glass window with a ring in his pocket. It's the contrast of his black soul in a holy space, of winning the heart of a man so cruel. It's my girlhood fantasy, the white day and the big dress. It's imagining saying yes.

"Miss Hart?"

I give a start.

A woman with a clipboard breezes past me. "Your models are ready. You're on in ten."

I jump back into action. My dream dissolves in a flurry of activity. The model wearing my day dress cusses when the zipper gets stuck. I work on it while she fixes her lipstick.

"Maxime fucking Belshaw is out there," she says, dabbing powder onto her nose.

"What?" With the noise, I'm not sure I heard correctly.

"God, I hope I catch his eye." She fits her shoes.

"Hart, you're on," the organizer calls from the stage door.

"That's us," the model says, making her way over.

The rest passes in a blur. It's crazy and exhilarating. It's so damn stressful, and I love every minute. I run on pure adrenaline by the time the wedding dresses are paraded. Standing backstage with the rest of my class, I revel in the moment our ultimate creations are revealed on the runway. For an unreal moment, I lose myself in the lights and music as my eyes follow that dress, knowing it's perfect because I made it for *him*.

I search the crowd until I find Maxime. He sits in the front row on the left. The stage lights illuminate his face, making the shadows under his eyes run deep. The groove between his eyebrows begs me to trace the line and drag a finger over the bump at the bridge of his crooked nose. His eyes are bright with pride and his lips pulled into the slightest of smiles. I turn hot knowing what those lips have said and done to me, knowing how deft those strong, slender fingers are. I love watching him like this, when he's unaware and his guard is down, but then there's applause and Madame Page gets on the stage.

I miss most of her speech, my thoughts being scattered in every direction. I'm rerunning the show in my mind. I should've pulled out the seam and re-stitched the body. My head is spinning with everything I've realized tonight. I can't look away from Maxime's face or strong body. I imagine his broad chest and well-cut muscles underneath his shirt. All I want right now is to straddle him and claim him as my very own forever.

Someone takes my hand—Christine—and we form a line to walk

onto the runway. I take my bow like the rest, feeling like somehow this is a dream, and the only real thing is Maxime in his tux, looking as if he may eat me alive.

We stand on stage as the judges call their verdicts. The panel is made up of a mix of fashion editors, designers, and label owners. One by one, our average scores out of ten are called. Seven for Thérèse. Eight for Christine. Loud applause. Six for someone else. Four for another. One for me.

One.

It hits me like a bucket of ice water. The shock travels from my head to my toes, freezing its path down my limbs. I feel the blood drain from my face in shame. Automatically, my gaze finds Maxime's. His jaw bunches, but his gray eyes are sympathetic.

It's over. I blew it. I'm out. I'm not entering the next level. I'm not going to graduate or become a fashion designer. Worse, I suck. The panel agreed. Their decision is irreversible.

We bow. I smile like is expected of me, but inside I'm burning and freezing in interchanging bouts of humiliation and disappointment. I'm devastated. All those hours. All that magic I felt when I held my pencils and needles. All gone.

"Sorry," Christine whispers in my ear. Her eyes glitter when I meet her gaze. "Maybe next time."

The rest of my classmates enjoy their well-deserved glory as family members come up to congratulate them. I escape to the garderobe and start gathering my equipment.

"Hey," Maxime says behind me.

I soak up his warmth as he folds his arms around me from behind and presses his nose in my neck.

"Yours is my favorite," he says. "I'm proud of you, little flower. You've outdone yourself."

Turning in his embrace, I put my arms around his neck. "Don't lie to make me feel better."

He takes my hand and places it over his heart. "I promise. Cross my heart."

And hope to die. "Thank you."

His eyes are filled with understanding. "Shall we get out of here?"

"God, yes."

"Gather your stuff. I'll pack your dresses."

I'm so grateful to him right now. It doesn't matter that he got me into the course by pulling strings. I'm just happy he's here for me. I'm happy he's here when I need him most.

CHAPTER 19

Zoe

It takes me a few days to get over my disappointment. I hang my collection in a closet in one of the spare rooms where I don't have to look at it, but the knowledge that it's there remains. Every time I walk past that room, my failure screams at me.

By the end of the week, I pack everything into a box and donate it to charity, everything except for the wedding dress. I can't get it out of my heart to part with it, not after I've realized what it means. I only hang the dress deeper in the closet, hiding it in a black dry-cleaning bag.

On Saturday, I wander around aimlessly for a while, not having to work on anything for the first time in months. It's a cold, gray day with clouds rolling in from the sea. I try to read in the tower, but the wind howls around the corners.

Hold on. I know why I'm so listless. I've left the debacle about dropping out of fashion school unfinished. There's something I need to do.

I go downstairs to look for Maxime and find him behind his desk in his study. The door stands open. Lines of worry run over his forehead and around his eyes. He's so engrossed in his work he doesn't notice me. I knock because he still keeps the room locked, which means I'm not welcome inside.

He looks up and smiles. "I've just been thinking about you."

"You have?" I wave at the groove between his eyebrows. "It doesn't look like pleasant thoughts."

"Come here."

I pad over the floor to his desk. "I know you're busy, but I just wanted to say thank you."

He gets to his feet and rounds the desk. "For what?"

"For making the fashion school possible. I just realized I never thanked you. I'm sorry for being so rude."

A fresh frown meets his smile. "I didn't take you for being rude, but I appreciate your gratitude." He shoves a hand into his pocket. "You're welcome."

I study him. He seems oddly formal this morning. It's not like him not to touch me when we're standing so close together. Usually, he can't keep his hands off me. He's always looking for excuses to kiss and fondle me. On any other morning, he would've had his hands on my hips and his mouth on mine by now.

"Okay," I say, swiping a strand of hair behind my ear.

"For whatever it's worth, I think you deserve—"

I hold up a hand. "You don't have to make me feel better. I did my best."

"There are other schools."

I shake my head. "It's fine." Madame Page proved her point. I don't have what it takes.

"I know how disappointed you are. You haven't been out of the house since the fashion show."

I glance at the window. "The weather hasn't been good."

"I think you need to get out, Zoe."

"Get out where?"

"Go to a movie. Do some shopping. Have your hair done. Whatever makes women feel good."

"You mean alone?" Except for meeting Sylvie and going to school, he's never let me go anywhere alone. As Sylvie and I haven't spoken since the night I discovered her deceit, I've only been out to school on my own.

"I have a meeting. There's no reason why you should be cooped up in the house." He reaches out, hesitates, and finally cups my cheek. "Go on before I touch you more and change my mind."

The opportunity is too rare not to jump at it. I can take a long walk on the jetty and lick my wounds in solitude. Alone time sounds exactly like what I need.

"Thank you," I say, my heart warming with gratitude.

"Dress warmly and no chatting to my men. They're there to protect you, which they can't do if a pretty woman distracts them."

I roll my eyes. "Yes, Dad."

His gaze heats. "Are you sassing me, Miss Hart?"

"Maybe."

"I'll have to pull you over my lap for that when you get back."

I go on tiptoes to kiss him. "I look forward to that."

He regards me with amusement as I backtrack to the door, the controlling and possessive Maxime silent for once.

"Do I have a curfew?" I ask, pausing in the frame.

"Just let me know where you are. I'll be busy until late afternoon. You don't have to be back before dinner."

There's something intense about him as he watches me leave. It's as if he's fighting with himself to let me go.

I put on my coat and scarf. Making sure my telephone is charged, I drop it with some money into my bag. I always have a stash of cash, courtesy of Maxime. He calls it my emergency fund, as if he doesn't already take care of my each and every need.

Outside, Benoit jumps to attention.

"What are you doing out here?" I ask. "Aren't you freezing?" I wasn't planning on going anywhere. He didn't have to hang around on a Saturday.

"Nah." He rubs his hands together. "I was running errands for Maxime."

"I'm going into town."

"My car or yours?"

"I'm taking some me time." I flash him a smile. "I'm driving alone."

He curses under his breath, hurrying to the Mercedes when I hop into the new Mini Cooper Maxime has bought for me. Two guards follow in his steps.

Throwing the car into gear, I leave the gates before Benoit has had time to start his engine. I grin as I look in the rearview mirror. His wheels are kicking up gravel in his attempt to catch up with me. I can try to shake him off and maybe even succeed, but I do feel better that he's tailing me. No matter how many times I tell him I don't need him, I appreciate the protection.

I take the scenic route. I enjoy driving, and it gives me time to think. However, today I don't find joy in the view or having this time to myself. That strange listlessness from earlier is still there. Something is bothering me. The notion is faint but persistent, like a dull headache or queasy stomach.

Determined to make the best of the time Maxime has granted me, I put my thoughts aside and drive to the main beach in Marseille. The parking is empty. So is the jetty. I'm happy to have the space to myself.

I button my coat up and pull the hoodie over my head against the cold wind. Benoit mutters some cusswords and says something about freezing his ass off as he follows me to the pier. From there, he lets me go alone. I walk all the way to the end. A spray of saltwater blows against my face. A seagull calls out, swooping low and landing in the swell.

I take my phone from my bag and send Maxime a text to let him know where I am. Benoit always lets him know, but texting him my whereabouts is one of Maxime's unbreakable rules. I don't want him to get it into his head to come looking for me just because I disobeyed, or worse, take away my freedom and privileges.

Holding my phone in my hand, I wait for it to vibrate with his reply. Nothing. I check the screen. The tick mark shows my message has been delivered, but the dots don't dance to indicate he's busy typing. That's strange. He always texts me back immediately. I wait a few more seconds, my unease growing, and finally pocket my phone.

It's not like him to ignore my messages. No matter where or when, I always get a reply. Come to think of it, Maxime behaved very out of character this morning. Letting me stand here alone like this is definitely not like him. No matter how much work or how many meetings he has, he never lets business get in the way of spending time with me on the weekends. If he has to attend an event, he takes me along. If I need to get out, he puts everything on hold to accompany me. I've always credited his behavior to making sure I don't escape, but maybe there's more to it. Maybe he's been considerate because he cares.

Then why is today is the exception? It doesn't make sense. He seemed so reluctant for me to go. Did something happen? Is that why he looked so worried? Is that why he's having such a long meeting on a Saturday? He's having it at home?

Wait. That look on his face when I left—the concern and eagerness—wasn't because he didn't want me to go. He couldn't wait to get rid of me.

Every instinct I own goes on high alert. That's what's been eating at me all the way here. Something is wrong, and it's bad.

Turning, I rush back up the pier.

Benoit straightens at my hurried approach, a half-eaten sandwich in his hand. Alarm flashes across his face. "Miss Hart?"

I run past him, pressing the remote to unlock my car.

"Zoe," he calls after me. "Zoe, wait." When I get behind the wheel, he throws down the baguette and runs for the Mercedes. "Fuck!"

I push down on the gas, breaking the speed limit. The Mercedes battles to keep up. My phone rings. Maxime? I yank it from my pocket and check the screen. Benoit. I cut the call and dump it on the seat, calling Maxime on voice command, but the phone goes straight to his voicemail.

Shit. What's happening? Something feels awfully wrong. He sent me away for a reason. For my safety?

My phone rings again. Benoit. I reject the call and drive faster. I think about calling Francine and asking her to check on Maxime, but then I remember it's her weekend off.

My nerves are shot by the time the house comes into view. My hands are shaking when I cut the engine and throw the car door open. The Mercedes races through the gates, Benoit coming to a hard stop behind me. He jumps from the car as I'm racing up the steps, catching up with me just as I grip the handle of the front door.

"Zoe." He grabs my wrist. "Stop."

I look at where he's touching me. "Let go." Maxime will cut his hand off for this.

"Fuck," he groans, releasing me. "Zoe, listen. Don't go in there."

Pushing the door open, I walk inside. I stop in the entrance and listen, expecting gunshots or fighting. What greets me is much worse.

Soft, feminine laughter.

The sound hits me like an arrow in the heart. Nausea rushes through my body. My stomach burns with it.

Maxime's voice reaches my ears. I can't hear what he's saying, but his tone is pleasant. The woman replies, then laughs again.

I follow their voices to the library and stop in the open door. Maxime sits on the couch and a woman with auburn hair and honey-colored eyes sits in the armchair in front of the fire, in *my* armchair, the chair in which Maxime has stripped me naked, draped me over his lap, and made me come more times than I can count. She's impossibly young and beautiful, cultured like his mother, wearing a dress Madame Page will approve of.

It only takes him a second to become aware of my presence. We're attuned to each other. That's what happens when you live together for thirty months. I know he hates lemon juice, and he knows I love sun-dried tomato salad dressing. He has to know this is killing me.

Maxime's expression is stoic. He holds my eyes unfalteringly. The woman is still talking, her voice ringing through the space in a well-groomed Parisian accent, not foreign like mine. There's no funny pronunciation to tease her about or to find endearing. She's perfect. Then she catches on and follows his gaze.

At the sight of me, her back snaps straight. She drags her eyes over me, taking in my Mary Poppins coat and sticky-salty, windblown hair.

Leaning her hands on the armrests, she pushes to her feet. "You *will* get rid of her. I will *not* be humiliated."

Maxime stands.

Picking her bag up from the foot of the chair, she walks past me with a lifted chin. I stare after her, familiar and new pain braiding together, twisting my insides. I know the ache of betrayal. I know the ache of having your life stolen but this...This is new. This is huge. I can't even find a box for it in the wall that makes up my soul. I can't file it with lies or betrayal. Not even jealousy is an accurate description. It cuts much deeper, leaving scars that will never heal.

Silence stretches through the house when she closes the door behind her like a well-bred lady. Me, I would've slammed it. Only her perfume lingers. Expensive. Classy. Everything I'm not. And the memory of that laugh. The torture of imagining what Maxime had said to her to make her so happy.

The silence is infuriating. I want him to explain. I want him to make excuses. I want him to tell me it's a misunderstanding, that she's his cousin or long-lost sister.

I take in his passive stance, how his hands are shoved deep into his pockets and his eyes give nothing away. Always hiding secrets. Never playing open cards with me. Waiting for me to make the first move. It's unfair, but his silence leaves me no choice.

"Who is she?" I ask in a tremulous voice.

"Izabella Zanetti, Leonardo Zanetti's sister." He holds my gaze, not as much as flinching when he says, "My fiancée."

CHAPTER 20

Zoe

The world crashes down around me. I didn't think it was possible to die and still be alive. I didn't think I could be in hell right here on earth. Yet the flames lap at me, mocking me yet again for my stupid naivety.

"The Italian I met at the auction?" I force through the lump in my throat. "That Leonardo?"

"Yes," Maxime says.

I curl my fingers until half-moons from my nails cut into my palms. The pain is the only thing preventing me from breaking down in tears. "How long?"

"My father made a deal."

My voice rises. "How long, Maxime?"

"The engagement party is next Saturday."

I inhale once, twice, trying not to show him how hard it is to breathe, how this minces me up inside. "Is that what you were discussing?"

"Yes." He adds in a flat voice, "Among other things."

I guess other things meaning the wedding. Oh, my God. I'm going to be sick. How long has he been playing me? "For how long have you known?"

"I don't think that matters."

My pulse jumps. Betrayal and humiliation turns to anger. "Don't you dare, Maxime Belshaw. Don't you dare tell me my feelings don't fucking matter. Tell me! You owe me at least this much."

"Two years." He gives me a resigned look. "The contract was signed two years ago."

Fuck. God, that hurts. I stumble back a step. "You made a fool of me."

"No, Zoe. You're not a fool."

"Don't you fucking say my name." I hold up a shaking finger. "Don't you fucking dare."

He takes a step toward me. "I didn't want you to find out like this."

"When were you planning on telling me?"

Another step. "This doesn't change anything."

I take three more steps back. "Like hell it doesn't!"

"We'll still be together, Zoe. Marrying Izabella is a business transaction."

"When?" I manage through trembling lips.

"In spring."

"In April?" I cry out. "You're marrying her in four months?"

"You'll still be my mistress. I'll still spend the majority of my time with you."

I think I'm going to break down, after all. I bite on the inside of my cheek until the urge to turn hysterical passes. "You'll fuck her."

"Only to create an heir."

"To make a baby." My teeth chatters around the words.

"Yes," he says with a frown, as if he's having a hard time understanding why I should be upset about that.

"What about us, Maxime? Have you considered that? What if I wanted a baby?"

"You know I can't do that."

Swallowing my tears, I lift my chin. "Why?"

"Bastard children aren't recognized. I won't be able to protect it with my surname. More so, bastard kids have a hard time adapting. They always come second. That's not fair to any child."

Does he even realize how far his selfishness goes? "And how are you supposed to get rid of me before this marriage?" I ask, repeating his *fiancée's* words.

For the first time, he has the decency to look guilty. "Naturally, as my wife, Izabella will live here."

"So, you're throwing me out." I backtrack to the stairs. "I'll start packing, then. I'll be glad to go home."

He comes after me so fast I don't have time to run. His fist is in my hair before my foot is on the second step of the stairs.

"I'm not throwing you out," he growls against my ear, "and I'm not sending you home."

"I'm not sleeping with an engaged or married man. There's no point in keeping me. You'll have to take what you want with force, but I refuse to be the other woman."

His hold tightens in my hair, making my scalp sting. "Marriage has nothing to do with sex and love. Not in my world. If I want our business to survive, I don't have a choice but to honor that contract and marry Izabella. I'll respect her and care for her as my wife, but it's you I want."

"I can't do this, Maxime. You have no right to ask this of me."

His voice turns cruel. "Oh, but I'm not asking, little flower."

"Fuck you," I cry, pulling so hard his hand comes free from my hair with the long strands stuck to his fingers.

"Maybe it's a good idea to start packing, after all." He reaches for me, but I jump away. "In time, you'll get used to the idea."

"Never," I bite out. "Not as long as I live."

"That's how you felt at first, but you got used to this." He waves a hand around the space. "You're a survivor. You'll adapt."

I can't listen to him anymore. I escape up the stairs, and he lets me. The only mercy he gives me is not coming after me. I keep on moving until I run out of stairs. Rushing into the tower, I shut the heavy door behind me. There's no key to guarantee my solitude. The only door in this house with a key is Maxime's study. That's where he locks away his laptop and the phones, any form of communication with the outside world. My passport has to be in there. I have to find it.

Sitting down on the window seat, I wrap my arms around myself. I'm cold. Shivering. Finally, the tears I'm trying so hard to swallow erupt. They escape with ugly wails of shameless, pitiful crying. I focus my blurry gaze on the distorted vision through the stained glass window. The color twists through my tears like a kaleidoscope. The sounds of footsteps falling on the stairs makes me suck in and hold my breath. The sob trapped between my ribs aches, but I keep it in with all my might. I can't let anyone see me like this, least of all not Maxime.

A knock falls on the door. "Zoe?"

I can't answer. If I do, he'll hear my brokenness. I'm not giving him that much.

"I'm coming in," he says.

I swallow, somehow finding inhumane strength to keep my voice even. "If you care about me at all, even just a little, you won't."

Silence. After a beat, he says, "I'm going to my parents' house. I'll be back for dinner."

"To see her?"

"To smooth things over. She's upset."

No shit. Pulling my legs up, I wrap my arms around my knees.

"Benoit stays here," he says, "in the house."

Another silence. Finally, after a long stretch of waiting, his heels tap an even rhythm on the stairs as he descends.

I let out the breath I was holding. My chest expands with another sob. Suddenly, I'm not sure whose cruelty is worse, Alexis's or Maxime's. Maxime knew all along while he was fucking me and being kind to me, watching me fall for him a little more each day, that he was promised to someone else. This is my limit. This is the straw that breaks the camel's back and sends me over the edge.

Wiping my nose with the back of my hand, I rest my head against the cold stones of the wall and close my eyes. No wonder Maxime's family hates me so much. It all makes sense now. I'm the imposter, the seducer, and the mistress. They're the wives. I think back to a conversation I once had with Sylvie when I still thought we were friends. It was over a glass of wine after class. We talked about made men and how they treated their women. I wanted to know more about what it meant to be property since it had become my label in Maxime's world.

"It usually goes hand in hand with big depth payoffs that can't be honored," Sylvie had said.

The revelation shouldn't have startled me. Still, her words shocked me. "Like selling a person to settle a debt?"

"Or making big, financial sacrifices for a woman. Taking care of her for life."

It sounded too savage to be true. "Why not just marry? Why use such a degrading term?"

"Property isn't degrading. It's a coveted and protected position. It means hands-off to all other men. Whoever dares to touch a man's property is dead. Marriages are made for the business, to further relationships that'll profit the family. Men seldom want or love their wives. As you can imagine, there are a lot of mistresses going around in our circles. Us girls, the ones who are expected to remain virgins and marry a man of our father's choice for the sake of a contract, don't get to be mistresses. We get to remain faithful and suffer their existence pretending we don't notice. Of the lot, I'd say we're the worst off."

She was wrong. They get to be respected. They get to go out with their husbands in public. They're not hidden away somewhere, only taken out of their golden cages on occasion for a quick, dirty weekend in a hotel with mirrors on the ceiling. Maxime won't be able to take me to his events any longer. Izabella will be on his arm. I'll wait alone for the crumbs of his time, tucked away like a cheesy princess dress in a black dry-cleaning bag, a hidden secret in a dark closet. Among women, only the wives are recognized. That's why Maxime never introduced me to the wives when he hoped I'd make friends. That's why I only got to mix with the women who didn't wear diamonds on their ring fingers. No, the wives are much better off. The wives get to have the babies. That is maybe the worst, the part that twists the blade the deepest into my heart.

I sit there until my stomach protests with hunger pangs and my throat is so dry it's hard to swallow. The day turns dark. The tower is freezing cold. Pressing the heels of my palms against my eyes, I rub away the tears. I feel dry and empty. I won't let Maxime find me like this. He's bound to be home soon. I can't even let myself think about what's happening at his parents' house. It hurts too much.

The door squeaks when I open it. I listen. The house is quiet. I walk down the stairs into the deserted darkness, not bothering to flick the lights on or turn the heat up. I walk straight to Maxime's study and test the door. Locked. I have to find a way in. If only I knew how to pick a lock.

I walk to the kitchen and stop in the door. Benoit sits at the window counter with a mug in front of him, reading something on his phone.

He looks up. "Jesus, Zoe."

I hold up a palm. "Don't speak."

He knew. They all knew. Everyone knew and no one bothered to tell me. They're all on Maxime's side. I'm on my own in this, always have been. Just like Damian has always said. Why didn't I listen to him? Why did I prefer to cling to stupid fantasies?

"There's coffee," Benoit says. "You look like you can do with some."

I take a glass from the cupboard and fill it with water from the tap. Taking aspirin from the cupboard where Francine stores the sugar cubes, I drink it for the throbbing pain in my head. Crying always does that to me.

I pop a piece of bread in the toaster, ignoring Benoit's stare as I take butter and jam from the fridge. When I open the drawer to take a butter knife, I pause. The slot for the sharp vegetable knives is empty. I look at the knife block on the counter. All the bread and carving knives are gone. Even the scissors.

Benoit clears his throat. "Maxime thought it was better to lock the knives away."

He thought I'd try to kill him? Harm myself? No, that's not my plan. That's not who I am. An image of Damian and me sitting with our knees drawn up in a dark closet with only a flashlight and a book filters into my mind. I hear the fighting and glasses breaking. I feel the cold fear of violence. I hear my brother's voice, telling me our circumstances don't define us.

Maxime was right about one thing. I'm a survivor. I'm going to follow Damian's advice.

I'm going to save myself.

CHAPTER 21

Zoe

By the time Maxime gets home, I've moved my clothes and toiletries to one of the spare bedrooms, the one the farthest away from the one meant for his wife.

I'm in bed when he knocks on the door. I stay on my side with my face turned to the wall and my eyes closed. Porcelain clatters as his footsteps near. There are no fancy rugs or carpets in this room, only a cold, barren stone floor, just the way I prefer. It reminds me I'm in his prison, not in his home.

A whiff of roses reaches my nostril.

"I brought you a cup of tea," he says.

The cup and saucer click on the nightstand. The mattress indents as he sits down on the edge. When he strokes a broad palm over my hair, I cringe. He withdraws the touch.

"No one can change what you mean to me, Zoe," he says. "You make me feel things I've never felt before. When you touch me, I'm alive. You're the only person in this world who makes me see light.

The only good I have inside me is when you're around." He pauses. "There's not much I can deny you. You know that. I'll make you happy again. I promise."

I turn on my back and open my eyes. His face is beautiful in its imperfection. It's a face I hold dear to my heart, but I won't let him hurt both me and the woman who's been promised to him. I won't be the reason for making another woman suffer the way I'm suffering now.

"If you want to make me happy," I say, "let me go."

"I'll give you anything in my power, but not that."

"There's no point in keeping me. I'm not a cheater. I'm not going to sleep with you."

"We'll go to Venice."

"Venice?" I bite out. "Do you think that place holds any good memories for me?"

He flinches. "Making love for the first time isn't a good memory?"

"You stole my virginity with manipulation." My tears threaten to spill over again. "You stole my love knowing you belonged to another. There's no place in the world you can take me to make me forget that."

"Where's the girl who believed in love and romance?"

"I don't believe in fairytales any longer."

He cups my cheek. "But you want to."

I turn my face away, escaping the touch. "Please. Leave me."

He considers me for a moment, then stands. Staring down at me, he says, "I'll give you time to get used to the change." After another stretch of silence, he walks to the door. In the frame, he turns. "Drink your tea. You'll feel better."

When he's gone, I grab the cup and hurl it at the wall. It breaks with a shattering sound into pieces, the rose petal infusion wasted on the floor.

I DON'T SLEEP that night. I lie awake in the dark, thinking. At daybreak, I have a shower and dress in my favorite leggings and jersey. I brush my hair and put on my makeup. I eat breakfast in the knife-less kitchen. I clear out the room Maxime turned into a workspace for me, packing the fabric, buttons, lace, ribbons, and thread into boxes that I seal. Benoit helps me to carry them down to the cellar. I vacuum and air the room, getting rid of my presence and smell. I make sure there's no traces left of me, nothing that can hurt another woman. All that's left when I'm done is my sewing machine. I seal it in its original box and make Benoit carry that to the cellar, too.

By the end of the week, the armchair in the library has been replaced with a new one I've ordered online. The old one I've burned on the beach. Maxime says nothing through it all. He gives me the space he's promised. His guards avoid me. They avert their eyes when I go outside for a walk. Even Francine isn't cruel enough to say she told me so. Like everyone else, she keeps her distance. They're avoiding me as if I'm on death row.

On Wednesday, Maxime comes to find me in my new room. He's holding my coat and scarf in his hand.

"Come on," he says. "We're going for a ride."

"Where to?"

"You'll see."

We haven't spoken since the night he promised to give me time, but I haven't stopped thinking. My thoughts haven't been quiet for a moment. There's something I need to know.

"If Damian doesn't honor the deal you have with Dalton, what are you going to do to him?"

His expression becomes closed-off again. "Whatever it takes."

"That's your plan? That's why you're keeping me? To use me against him?"

"I already told you why I'm keeping you." He holds the coat open. "Come now. You're going to like what I want to show you."

"If you didn't have me, what else would you use?"

He sighs. "There's always someone or something a person cares about."

"You'll hurt him or whoever and whatever he cares about to have your way."

"In short, yes."

I nod. That's what I needed to know.

"Zoe, please. Don't make me put this coat on you. I want this day to be pleasant."

Too late. Pleasant is no longer an option for us. Maybe he should've just given me to Alexis. It would've saved his future wife and me a lot of tears. Turning, I let him help me into the coat and stand obediently while he winds the scarf around my neck.

"That's better," he says with a soft smile.

I follow him to his car, but get in before he can get my door. I don't ask where we're going. For now, I simply go along. He follows the highway to the city and weaves his way through the narrow streets toward the center. Close to the old town, he parks. We make our way on foot through the pedestrian area until he stops in front of a beautiful, old building.

"This is it," he says, looking up at the stone façade. "It dates from 1000 BC."

I have no interest in the history of the building or why we're here. The guards who followed check the street before he punches a code into the panel that opens the street door. We climb all four levels of a winding staircase to the top and exit in a long, narrow corridor with a red carpet and a carved wooden door at the end.

"Here," he says in front of the door, handing me a key with a red ribbon tied through the hole in the top.

I take the cold metal, letting the silk ribbon slide through my fingers.

"Open it," he says.

Inserting the key in the lock, I turn it like he's told me.

"Go on," he says, placing his palm on the small of my back. "Go inside."

I open the door and step inside not because I want to, but to escape his touch. It smells of fresh paint. Pausing just inside the door, I look around. It's a loft apartment, beautifully renovated to leave the antique stone walls bare. A round window with stained glass panels dominates the ocean-facing wall. It stretches all the way from the ceiling to the floor. The floors are polished stone. White mohair rugs are scattered around. All the furniture in the open-space living area is white—the leather sofas, the velvet armchair, the whitewashed table, and the renaissance chairs. Each chair is of a different style, covered with a different white fabric, the textures and weave patterns adding uniqueness while the white gives uniformity. Only the backs are upholstered with fabric portraying images of different flowers in creamy beige.

A wrought iron spiral staircase leads to an open landing with a desk and chair. A study. A bookshelf stretches from the floor of the lounge to the ceiling of the study. The shelves are filled with English and French books, the titles ranging from classics to modern fiction and non-fiction. My gaze falls on The History of Fashion from the Middle Ages. For easy access, a ladder on wheels is hooked to the top shelf. There's a reclining chair and reading lamp under the stairs. Sofas and a low coffee table are arranged around a fireplace with carved flowers on the mantelpiece.

The kitchen takes up the right-hand side of the space. The cupboards are whitewashed and the appliances stainless steel. Through the glass panels on the doors, crockery in pink and gray are visible. Even the wine glasses are a deep pink with roses decorating the crystal stems. A huge bouquet of pink roses stands in an antique white vase on the island counter that serves as a more informal table with two tall chairs.

A door leads off to the right. My feet carry me there, compelling me to take it all in. It's a bedroom. The king-size bed is covered with white linen and pink scatter cushions. The French doors open onto an ornate waist-high rail. The windows face the building opposite the narrow street. White organza curtains provide privacy.

A door leading from the bedroom gives access to a well-organized dressing room with ample cupboard space. Another door opens into a windowless bathroom with Harlequin white-and-black tiles and a skylight allowing natural light. There's a spa bath like at Maxime's house and a shower with double nozzles. The vanity area is spacious with a big mirror and a padded stool. The bedroom, dressing room, and bathroom run along the back of the kitchen. It's huge. One room. For one person. Maybe for a partner who sleeps over on occasion. No rooms for children or visiting family.

Up to now, Maxime has let me take it all in silently, following quietly behind me. I catch his gaze when I turn to exit the bathroom.

His tone is eager. "There's more. Come."

He walks ahead of me to the French doors opening from the living area out to a terrace. We exit from the warm interior into the frosted winter air. My breath is a white puff as I exhale. A splash pool, Jacuzzi, and small summerhouse take up the ocean side. A vine creeps over the metal awning that will provide shade in summer. Potted olive trees frame the summer house and another stands next to a small garden table and two wrought iron chairs. Big pots with winter flowers are arranged around the space to form a terrace garden. A glass greenhouse filled with neatly arranged plants in terracotta pots is constructed on the left. I spot cherry tomatoes, chilies, carnivorous plants, and orchids through the glass.

"What do you think?" Maxime asks behind me.

"It's beautiful," I say honestly. He must've invested a fortune in this place. I turn to face him. "Did you have the renovations done?"

"It took two years," he says proudly.

Two years. All the pain from Saturday comes tumbling out. "Ah. Well, I guessed you didn't just pop out and buy this place yesterday."

"No." His expression sobers as he studies my face. "I bought it two years ago."

He planned it all along. He knew he'd need a place to ship me to.

"The work is only just finished," he says.

Otherwise, he would've made me move in sooner.

"I'll have your clothes sent over," he continues. "A team will unpack everything. You won't have to lift a finger."

The hurt spreads and spreads until I breathe and exhale it, until my heart beats with it and my pulse pumps with it.

"So," I say, "this is the new golden cage."

"It's yours, Zoe. No one can ever take it away from you. The day anything happens to me, this apartment will belong to you together with enough money to allow you to live comfortably for the rest of your life."

I stare at him, my feelings adrift. My emotions won't let me make sense of anything. They won't let me form words.

He approaches tentatively, his arms spread out with his palms facing the heavens. "Will you at least let me hold you?"

The offer tears me to pieces. I need the solace. I so badly need for someone to hold me. Just for a minute. Just for a few seconds. But he belongs to another.

Biting back my tears, I shake my head.

I'm not a cheater, and he's not a rapist. He won't take me by force, not without my consent.

He drops his arms. "I'll let you settle in, then. The fridge is stocked. If you need anything, you only have to call."

The agony is so complete I want to sink to my knees under its force. A silent scream catches in my chest when he turns his back on me and walks through the door. I can only stand there while he rips my life apart with his kindness.

CHAPTER 22

Zoe

It takes me a while to come to my senses. I'm frozen from cold when my limbs finally obey the signals from my brain to move. The first thing I do is go to the front door and yank it open. A man stands on attention in the corridor. My spirits sink. Of course.

"Babysitting?" I ask like a bitch.

"I'm here to protect you, ma'am, and to let Mr. Belshaw know if you need anything."

"What if I need to go out?"

"Your car will be delivered shortly, but you're not to go anywhere without Mr. Belshaw's permission. I'm to accompany you." He adds, "For your safety."

"Where's Benoit?"

"He's driving your car over, but he's no longer your appointed detail."

I suppose Benoit is Maxime's best man. He'd be protecting Maxime's wife.

I shut the door in his face and let my handbag drop from my shoulder to the floor. Crouching down, I turn it upside down, shaking the contents out over the polished stone. I gather all the loose bills, and then the ones in my purse. I have enough money for a plane ticket to Spain. I can disappear from there, but I need my passport.

Sitting down with my back resting on the wall, I bite my nail. I have to get into Maxime's study. I've seen him taking guns from a safe in his room, but there weren't any documents inside. It has to be locked somewhere in his study. Maybe now that I'm no longer living in his house, he'll leave the door unlocked. Which means I only have to get into his house. I have to try, at least.

I scramble to my feet and open the door again. "When Benoit drops off my car keys, can you please ask him to say hi before he goes?"

He gives me an uncertain look.

"I just want to say goodbye. We've been through a lot."

Everyone knows about Gautier. The hard resolve on his face softens. "Fine."

I take my phone to the study and use a paperclip to force it open. After removing the battery, I replace the cover and drop the phone in my inside coat pocket. Then I make tea while I wait.

The doorbell rings an hour later. I open the door to Benoit.

"Your keys." He holds the car keys out to me.

"Thank you," I say, accepting them. "Is Maxime home?"

"He's at the office. Why?"

"I need you to drive me back to Maxime's place. I left my phone there."

He scratches his head. "I'll let Maxime know. He can drop it off."

"No," I say quickly. "He'll be angry with me. You know how he gets when I forget my phone." It's one of Maxime's nonnegotiable rules, especially after the drive-by shooting.

Benoit rubs the back of his neck. "I don't know."

"I'll be in and out. Come on. What am I going to do? Rob him? Please, Benoit. I don't want to get into trouble with Maxime. I'm in enough trouble as it is."

He glances over my shoulder. "Is the place all right?"

"It's lovely. Now will you help me?"

Taking his phone from his pocket, he says, "Maybe it's in your bag. Have you checked carefully?"

I cross my arms. "Of course, I have."

He scrolls down his screen and dials my number. "It's dead."

"Damn. The battery must've run flat."

He sighs. "Fuck. Fine. In and out. Understand?"

"Thanks, Benoit."

Benoit nods at the guard by my door. "No need to report this. We're just going back for her phone."

I swallow a sigh of relief as Benoit leads me to the underground parking and shows me my parking space.

"You'll need the card I left in your visor to lower the concrete pillars that block vehicles from using the pedestrian area," he explains. "Only residents are allowed on these roads."

We get into the Mercedes. My nerves are all over the place. I can't stop myself from fiddling with the tussles of my scarf.

"You all right?" Benoit asks, shooting me a sideways glance.

"Just unsettled." When he frowns at me, I add, "With the change and all."

"Don't be too hard on yourself."

I'm not sure what that's supposed to mean. Don't beat myself up about cheating? Don't be upset about Maxime's upcoming engagement and wedding?

The usual guards are around when we stop at the house, but they don't ask questions. For all they know, Benoit is acting on Maxime's instructions.

Benoit stops in the entrance to take off his coat. I glance around the space in which I already feel like a stranger. It's as if my mind and heart know I'm no longer welcome, whereas my feet carry me along the familiar path to the library wing. Oh, thank God. The door to Maxime's study stands open, just as I hoped.

"Where did you leave it?" Benoit calls after me.

"I'm not sure. I think the last time I used it was in the library."

I listen for sounds of life before I enter. Only the faint clanging of pots and pans come from the kitchen on the other side of the house. There seems to be no one else except for us and Francine.

"Get a move on," Benoit says.

I turn over cushions and feel along the seams of the couch. "Do you mind checking in the kitchen? I don't feel like facing Francine."

"I thought you said you used it here."

"I think so, but I can't remember," I say, straightening. "Maybe I left it in the kitchen where I had breakfast."

"I should just tell Maxime to check the geolocation," he grumbles.

"Only as a last resort. Maxime will be furious with me."

I pretend to look around the desk, watching from under my lashes until he walks through the door. The minute he's gone, I tiptoe to the frame and peer around. When he rounds the corner, I rush to the study, trying to make as little noise with my heels on the floor as possible.

My heart beats wildly in my chest. If Benoit catches me, he'll definitely tell Maxime. There will be hell to pay. I'll lose whatever little freedom I have. Maxime will no doubt think up a cruel lesson to punish me, and I would've wasted the only opportunity I'll ever have of escaping.

Hurrying to his desk, I start at the most obvious place by going through his drawers. I yank open the top one and search through the neat stack of files. The second drawer holds old invoices and receipts, and the third stationary. My hope sinking, I go for the top drawer on the other side. More papers and files. Shit. My hand shakes uncontrollably as I pull open the second drawer. A notepad and diary. My breathing is staccato when I grip the handle of the last drawer. Please, God, let it be here. I pull, but the drawer is stuck. Something has bent upward inside, preventing it from sliding open. I look around on the desk, and settle on a ruler. Wiggling it through the small space at the top of the drawer, I manage to push down the papers blocking it and free the drawer. I almost pull it off its track when it finally gives.

Hurry, Zoe. Hurry.

I stick my hand inside, and then freeze. A stack of envelopes tied with a ribbon is pushed to the back of the drawer. That's what got stuck. The pile is so big it's higher than the drawer.

My breath catches. I can't drag air into my lungs. It's as if I've taken a punch in the stomach. I know what those letters are even before I pull the pile out and turn it to the light. My handwriting. Damian's address in jail.

Maxime never mailed them.

His words ring through my mind. *You can write to Damian as much as you like.*

He never said he'd send the letters. A clever choice of words. Just another sentence constructed to deceive me.

The betrayal stings. Tears burn behind my eyes. I didn't think I had more to shed. Untying the ribbon, I go through the pile. Every week, every letter—they're all here.

A door slams on the other side of the house.

I jump back to life, sniffing as I tie the undelivered words—empty words now, all my warnings worthless—back together and leave it exactly as I found it before closing the drawer.

"Zoe?" Benoit calls from up the hall.

I leave the ruler as it was before, neatly aligned with the desk calendar, and run from the study. I'm not going to make it back to the library. Benoit's footsteps are already falling too close. Slowing to a walk, I smooth down my hair, take my phone from my pocket, and inhale deeply.

Benoit rounds the corner and stops when he sees me, suspicion pulling his brows together.

"Found it," I say breathlessly, forcing a smile to my lips and holding the phone up for him to see. "I left it in the toilet."

He regards me narrowly. I don't know if he believes me, but finally he throws a thumb at the door. "We better get going. Maxime wanted me to bring your sewing machine."

"No, thanks," I say in an upbeat tone as I head for the door. "I don't need it any longer."

He follows me outside and gets into the car when I do.

"You shouldn't give up so easily," he says, starting the engine. "With the sewing, I mean."

"Oh, I'm not giving up." Not by a long shot. I'm only more determined to get away now than ever.

"Good."

Thankfully, he doesn't speak on the way back to the city. It gives me time to process what I've discovered. Damian must think I've abandoned him. He doesn't know his jail mate is his enemy. He doesn't know I've been taken and held against my will. He only knows what Maxime made me write on the fancy hotel stationary in Venice —that I ran away with a foreigner who swept me off my feet.

"You all right?" Benoit asks.

"Mm?" I look away from the ocean. "Yes."

"If you ever want to talk… Nah, what am I saying? I'm probably the last person you'd talk to."

I give him a smile. "I appreciate it, anyway."

"Make sure you charge your phone."

"Yeah."

"Don't let it happen again. Maxime won't like it."

"I know."

He pulls into the underground parking and insists on accompanying me to the door where the other guard is still positioned.

"We'll send a replacement in an hour," Benoit tells the man.

"Thanks, Benoit," I say again before shutting them both out behind the closed door.

Leaning on the cool wood, I drag in a few ragged breaths. I hate him. I hate Maxime with every fiber of my being. I hate him as much as my traitorous heart still loves him. This isn't puppy love. This isn't a fairytale kind of love. It's a love forged with thorns, pain, and suffering. It's a dark love, a habitat conducive to the growth of twisted lust like fungus favors damp places. It's a black stain over the crack in the wall of my heart, a wolf's face in a child's nightmare. It's a real love, a hard-earned love, the kind that lasts forever. I'll carry it inside me like a parasite for the rest of my life. I'll nurture it like a host unwillingly nurtures a cancer by breathing and eating. I'll suffer it like the unwanted burden it is, but I'll suffer it alone.

Pushing away from the door, I go to the foreign bathroom in the foreign space and strip naked. I fiddle with the settings of the shower until I figure out how to operate them and wash my body and hair. I dry off and pull on a robe.

My clothes arrive shortly. A team of three women unpack the rails full of dresses and boxes full of shoes. In under an hour, they're gone.

I go to the fridge and open it. There's rosé champagne and pink caviar, a dinner fit for a celebration. I choose the champagne. Popping the cork, I pour some in one of the beautiful crystal flutes with the glass roses creeping around the stem and walk to the circular window. I stare through the colored glass, but all I see are white envelopes and black ink.

The door opens and shuts.

Silence.

Pain.

When will it stop?

Will time alone ever be enough?

"Zoe."

His voice. I shiver. I hate him, and I want him. God, how I hate myself for needing him, even now. Especially now. He designed this. He made sure I have no one else to turn to. That's how he caught me in his beautiful web. I'm not letting him spin any more lies around me.

"I brought dinner. Chinese. I didn't think you'd feel like cooking."

I turn.

He's unpacking food cartons on the island counter. "What did you do with yourself this afternoon?"

"Why? Do you care?"

He lifts his gaze to mine. "You know I do."

I take a sip of champagne. "Nothing."

"I'm having a home gym delivered. There's space to put it in the dressing room."

I laugh. It's a nasty sound. "You want me to work out? Make sure I don't get fat from staying locked up in here all day?"

He takes two plates from the cupboard. "You don't have to stay locked up. You can go where you want as long as you let me know and my man goes with you."

"To check up on me and report back to you?"

"To keep you safe." He opens a carton and scoops noodles onto a plate. "I still have enemies. They'd still like to get to me through you."

"Don't remind me."

"Only for your safety." He tears a packet open with his teeth and pours sweet and sour sauce over my noodles the way I like. "I told Benoit to bring your sewing machine.

"I don't want it."

"You can putter around in the garden. That's why I had the greenhouse installed. I remembered the plant in your apartment."

"How considerate."

"You'll find plenty of good books. I got all the latest bestsellers. Romance. The flat screen I ordered wasn't ready today, but I'll make sure it's here by Monday. You'll have unlimited access to movies and those soapies you like."

"The news?"

"Not the news or any other channels."

"I suppose that means no laptop, either."

"The pool will make up for it in the summer. You can spend your days outside. There's a fully equipped gas barbecue in the summerhouse. It's easy to operate. I'll show you."

"I would've been happy with a shack, Maxime." No money in the world can buy me. "You shouldn't be here. It's wrong."

His face darkens. Pulling out one of the tall chairs, he says, "Come sit."

I pad over obediently and shift onto the chair.

Taking another flute, he pours himself a glass of champagne. "To your new home."

I don't raise my glass to his.

"I want you to be happy," he says.

Just like that. Like it's a button I can push. On. Off. God, I wish it was that easy.

"You should take up a hobby." He pushes the plate toward me and hands me a pair of chopsticks. "Painting or yoga. Journaling. Knitting. Anything you like."

"I'll keep that in mind."

He leans his elbows on the counter, putting our faces close. "In case you had any illusions about it, I'm staying the night."

It's like slap in the face. "This is what you call respect?"

He walks to the lounge and crouches in front of the fireplace. "This is where I'm supposed to be," he says, throwing a log into the empty fireplace, "and nothing about us is wrong."

I can't listen to it. I hop off the chair.

"Where are you going?" he asks, the darkness that's such an integral part of him surfacing in his voice.

"To the bathroom."

His gaze burns on my back as I walk to the bedroom and close the door behind me. Placing a hand over my stomach, I fight to calm my breathing. My heart thrums in my temples when I rush to the bathroom and go through my medicine box. A long time ago, right at the beginning of our *relationship*, Maxime got me sleeping pills. He thought it would help me to rest better. I've only taken one, and I hated how it made me feel. I was groggy in the morning, feeling worse than when I have a few hours of unmedicated sleep.

Pushing two of the pills out of their foil casing, I place them on the marble vanity, crush them with my hairbrush, and sweep the powder into the palm of my hand. Then I hurry back to the living area before my hands turn clammy from stress and the powder sticks to my skin.

Maxime is building a fire when I enter. He's busy enough with arranging the logs not to notice when I brush the powder into his glass. I give it a stir with my finger for good measure, and rub the rest of the residue that's stuck on my palm off on my robe.

When he returns, I take my seat and pick up my chopsticks. "Aren't you eating?"

He gives me an approving smile. "I wanted to make sure you were taken care of first."

I break the sticks apart and twist the noodles around one.

He grins. "Let me."

Leaning over me from behind, he arranges the chopsticks in my hand and manipulates my fingers to show me how to use them.

His voice is husky, his soft words and accent seductive against my ear. "Like this."

I inhale him, the clean smell of winter. The heat from his body penetrates my skin through my thick robe. I want him badly. I want to use him to take my pain away. I know he'll let me, but it's wrong to desire another woman's man. I stuff my mouth full of noodles. It's all I can do not to give in to temptation and tell myself it would be for old time's sake.

"You're angry with me," he whispers, running his nose along the line of my neck.

Goosebumps break out over my skin. It's a lot more complex than anger. What will he say if I confront him about the letters? He'd tell me he never lied. He'd say he told me I could write them. He never promised to mail them. He'd know I snooped around in his study, and he'd want to know why.

I swivel the chair away from his touch. I'm only a woman, and he makes me weak. The top two buttons of his shirt are undone. His tie sits askew, as if he's pulled on the noose. I trace the outline of his chest with my eyes, remembering every groove and outline that define his muscles. I commit this sin, taking with my eyes, but I can't look lower to where his manhood swells under the expensive fabric of his tailored pants.

"Eat with me," I beg. Anything to not let me give in to temptation. Our love and hate runs too closely together. Fucking, and hating, and loving have all become the same thing.

"Whatever my flower wants," he says, tracing my lips with a finger.

I lean away. "Please, don't," I say with a shaky breath. "Don't call me that, and don't touch me. I'm not ready."

To my relief, he drops his hand. When he takes the chair on the opposite side, the distance is my saving grace. I lift my glass. He does the same. I drink. So does he. I eat and drink, watching him do the same. He tells me we should have a picnic in one of the sheltered coves in summer. One of the coves. We can never swim on his private beach again. I haven't said goodbye to his house. The notion jars me. I never had time. Not enough to find closure. I listen while he talks, happy for him to make conversation for the both of us like only he can.

We finish the champagne in front of the fire sitting side by side on the sofa. Our bodies aren't touching, but I remember with longing how I used to curl up in his lap. The logs are almost burned out when he finally gets to his feet.

Yawning, he says, "I'm tired. Come to bed?"

"I'll be right there."

I wait for him to disappear into the bedroom before going through the pockets of his jacket where he's thrown it over the back of the sofa. No phone. I didn't expect as much. He usually carries it in the pocket of his pants.

I give it a good ten minutes before going to the room. Maxime is passed out in bed, snoring softly. One arm is thrown over his forehead, and the other is resting on his stomach. The nightstand is empty except for the lamp. There's no phone. I go to the dressing room. His clothes are neatly folded on the velvet bench. The sliding doors of the closets are open. Half of the space is filled with his shirts, pants, jackets, and shoes. He must've sent them with my things. I couldn't even pretend to be interested in how his team has organized our clothes. Maxime must've opened the closets to make sure they've done a good job.

Listening to be sure he's still snoring, I feel through the pockets of his pants. Shit. Nothing. I check in the bathroom. No phone. I go back to the room to check the nightstand again. Kneeling, I check under the bed and utter a soundless sigh of relief. He dropped his phone between the nightstand and the bed. He's really knocked out good.

After hastily pulling on a pair of socks, I touch Maxime's hand gently. He doesn't stir. I poke him a little harder. No reaction. Taking his thumb, I push it on the thumbprint button of his phone to unlock the screen, and then slip through the room to the living area. I can't go out into the hallway. The guard will be there. Instead, I pull the

French doors open as quietly as I can and close them behind me. The night is freezing cold.

It's not that late yet. With shaking fingers, I type the number for the correctional services where Damian is held and bite my nail as I wait for the call to connect. My body is shaking from more than the cold. If Maxime catches me, he'll punish me like never before.

"Johannesburg Correctional Services. May I help you?"

"I'd like to speak to Damian Hart, please."

"Sorry, ma'am. Calling hours are from nine to eleven am."

"It's a family emergency. May I leave a message?"

"Do you know his section?"

"A section."

"Hold on, please."

The line goes on hold. A song comes on. *Please, hurry.*

"Ma'am, he's been released on parole."

My mouth parts, but no sound comes out. I cough. "I'm sorry," I squeeze through my tight throat. "Can you tell me when?"

"Almost a year ago."

My lips go numb. "Thank you."

I cut the call. He got out. A year ago. Maxime didn't tell me. He has to know. He said he was keeping tabs on Damian. I clench the phone so hard the edges cut grooves into my skin. Before the screen goes dark, I call up an internet search page and type Dalton Diamond.

The page that comes up takes the wind from my sails. I read through it with growing disbelief. Dalton Diamonds has changed its name to Hart Diamonds after Damian Hart did a hostile takeover by acquiring the majority of the shares. I scroll to the contact section with growing panic, urgency spurring me on as I keep on glancing at the doors, expecting Maxime to storm through them any minute.

I open the icon. There's a contact form. Shit. My hand shakes so much I miss the menu button twice. I select *About the Owner*. There's a separate contact button at the end of that page. Saying a silent prayer, I click on it.

A number appears. A message pops up. *Would you like to connect?* I press yes.

A gruff voice comes on the line. "Damian Hart."

Oh, my God. I press a fist against my mouth to suppress a sob.

"Hello?" It sounds as if he's been sleeping.

"Damian?" I manage with an unsteady voice.

Alarm filters into his. "Who is this?"

"It's me, Zoe."

All traces of sleepiness vanish. He's wide awake now. "Zoe?"

I recognize the alertness and caution that are part of Damian's making. I don't waste time. I tell him, "I need your help."

"Where are you?"

"In France."

His tone is strong, reassuring. "What do you need?"

"I need you to get me out of the country. I'll need a passport. A false identity."

"Where's your nearest airport?"

"Marseille."

"How quickly can you get there?"

"Tell me when." I'll figure out a way.

"Hold on." There's a small pause. "There's a flight on Saturday morning at eleven."

"Perfect." Maxime will be occupied with his engagement party.

"I'll send a man. The name's Russell Roux. Tall, dark, and he'll wear a blue suit and red tie. The code word is apple pie. Meet him at the Air France information counter at eight."

"Okay."

"Can I reach you on this number?"

"No," I say quickly. "You can't call me again."

"Zoe, is there someone I need to take care of?"

I know what he means with *take care of*. "No. Just get me out of here."

"I'm bringing you home, Zee." He doesn't waste time with asking questions. "Whatever this is, we'll handle it."

"Thank you," I whisper.

There's caution in his tone. "Take care."

"See you soon."

I hang up, taking a moment to find my composure before wiping clean my search and call history. The apartment is quiet when I go back inside. Maxime is no longer snoring. My body breaks out in a coat of sweat. I drop his phone into the pocket of my robe and tiptoe back to the room, but he's still passed out in the same position.

Careful not to wake him, I shift the phone back between the nightstand and the bed on the floor. I take another shower to warm up and dress in a tracksuit before getting into bed. I stay well on the edge, far away from Maxime, but sometime during the night when I finally fall asleep, we find each other, because I wake up with his body pressed against my back and a heavy arm draped over my waist.

For a moment, I simply experience us. I take the memory and store it away.

I pretend to be asleep when he gets up. I don't stir while he's having his shower or gets dressed. I sense him staring down at me. I wait for him to call me out on my bluffing, but he only presses a kiss on my temple and quietly leaves.

The room turns colder in his absence. I guess it's something I'll have to get used to.

It's going to take me a while.

Goodbye, Maxime.

A sob catches in my throat. Since Maxime took me, I only wanted to get away. That first night in Venice, I never would've believed how completely I'd end up loving and hating him in equal measures. I never thought leaving him would be this hard or hurt this deeply.

CHAPTER 23

Zoe

I go through the motions. I dress, eat, and do the cleaning. I get through the day by potting around in the greenhouse and watering the plants. Like I expected, Maxime doesn't come to me after work. He's no doubt busy with the arrangements of tomorrow's party. He sends me a text to say he has a family obligation and will see me on Monday, that he will miss me and think about me every minute.

I read the text with mixed feelings through my tears. Sinking to my knees, I imagine him at his party with his strong body filling out his tux, and the look on his face as he slides a ring onto Izabella's finger in front of their families as witnesses. Will his smile be soft? Will his cold eyes warm for her? Will he give her the look of approval he saved for me when I dressed up for him? I let the thoughts punish me. I own the guilt and the pain. I carry the weight of the sin Maxime won't admit. Then I pick myself up from the floor and pack a bag.

I go to bed with the box of chocolates Maxime left in the kitchen cupboard, eating them all. I don't sleep. At five, I make the bed and tidy the apartment. I have a cup of coffee and a slice of toast. After a quick shower, I dress in a wool sweater and my favorite worn jeans. Then I pull a pair of baggy pants on over the jeans and fit my boots. Rolling my red thermal jacket into a small ball, I bundle it with a red beanie and scarf as well as my ballerina flats in my oversized handbag. I tie my hair into a ponytail, but don't apply makeup. I stare at my reflection in the mirror.

My eyes are dull and marred by dark rings. My cheeks are sunken, making my face look hollow. I don't bother with trying to disguise the feelings I wear on my sleeve with makeup. The worse I look, the more convincing I'll be with the guard.

At seven, I pull on my blue puffy jacket, take my car keys, and open the door. A different man from yesterday is on duty.

"Good morning," I say.

"Ma'am." His gaze runs over me. "Everything all right?"

"I need to get out."

He removes a phone from his pocket. "Where to?"

"Anywhere. I don't care."

He gives me a baffled look.

"Maybe the movies," I say. "Preferably a very long one."

Understanding passes over his face. It's the day of Maxime's engagement, after all. Any mistress would want to lose herself in a mindless activity to forget.

Typing something on his phone, he says, "I'm just letting Mr. Belshaw know."

"While we're at it," I say, going back inside and grabbing the bag, "I'll do my dry-cleaning." I dump the bag in his arms and then hand him the key to the apartment. "Do you mind?"

Not waiting to see if he follows, I walk down the hallway toward the elevator. The key sounds in the lock. He overtakes me and pushes the button, my bag slung over his shoulder.

When he holds the key out to me, I shake my head. "Please, keep it for me. I have a tendency to lose things when I'm distracted."

He gives a sympathetic nod. "Which cinema?"

"I don't care. Pick one."

We take my car. I drive while he checks the movie program on his phone. He gives me directions to a theatre near the harbor, someplace in Maxime's territory where we'll be safe.

I park in the underground parking of a shopping mall. I lock the bag in the trunk and ride the escalators up with the guard whose name I don't bother to ask. The earliest screening starts at ten. We're way too early. I buy two tickets at the self-service dispenser and go to a coffee shop to wait. The guard orders coffee. I ask for tea, a rose petal infusion. When the waitress puts the cup in front of me, it doesn't take much for genuine tears to flow.

"Excuse me," I say, wiping at my eyes and jumping to my feet. "I'm going to the bathroom."

The guard pushes to his feet, his eyebrows pulled together. "What can I do?"

"Please." I duck my head. "Just give me a moment."

He doesn't follow me to the bathroom, but moves his chair so that he has a view on the door. I push inside and rush to a stall. Locking the door behind me, I scramble out of my jacket, boots, and pants. I dump everything together with my phone in the trashcan before fitting my ballerina flats and the red thermal jacket.

Stepping out of the stall, I go to the mirror over the basins. I make quick work of untying my hair and shaking it out before fitting the beanie and pulling it low over my forehead. The final touch is adding sunglasses and bright red lipstick. For good measure, I shove my handbag under the sweater and zip up the jacket. I take a step back and study my reflection. I look like a different woman, at least nine months pregnant.

Forcing myself to take long, even breaths, I place a hand over my stomach and exit the bathroom. It takes everything I have to walk slowly like a woman late in her pregnancy instead of running. From behind the dark lenses of my glasses, I keep an eye on the guard. He's still watching the door, ignoring me. I hold my breath until I round the corner, and then I move.

I sprint down the escalator, yanking the bag out from under my sweater in the run. My lungs are burning by the time I reach the underground parking. I don't look left or right. I have the keys ready in my pocket. I push on the button to unlock the car. Only when I'm opening the door do I dare a glance at the doors giving access to the mall. All is quiet.

Shifting behind the wheel, I start the engine and get out of the parking area. Luckily, the first hour is free, so I don't have to waste time by paying. I only have to push the parking ticket into the slot for the barricade to open. I have no idea how much time I have. Maybe not long before the guard realizes I'm gone. Maxime will send men after me. He'll look for my car and license plate. At the nearest bus terminal, I park in an illegal spot and take my bag from the trunk. It won't take long before my car is towed away. Maxime will eventually find it at the impound, but hopefully it wins me more time.

I check the bus routes on the board, and take the number that goes to the airport. All the way there, my stomach twists so tightly I think I may be sick. I grip my handbag in my lap.

Please, God. Please.

After twenty minutes, the bus pulls up at the airport stop. I get out and fall in line with the other passengers, making sure I move in the middle of the group. I've never been to the airport, but it's not big. It doesn't take long to find the Air France information counter.

A tall man wearing a blue suit and red tie stands next to the counter, reading a tourist brochure. He's shorter than Maxime, but bulkier. One look at his strong frame tells me this man is in the security business. His brown eyes have that vigilant light that says he's aware of everything happening around him, even if he seems to be engrossed in what he's reading.

My assumption is proved correct when he looks up while I'm still a short distance away. Our eyes lock. He offers me a warm smile, the appreciative kind a man would only offer to a woman he knows well. He recognizes me. Maybe Damian showed him a photo.

I study his handsome face. He has deep laugh lines around his mouth and eyes. A bit of gray touches the russet color of his sideburns. He looks easygoing, yet alert, competent, exactly like someone Damian would trust and employ.

"Code word?" I ask under my breath as I stop in front of him, looking around to make sure we're not watched.

"Apple pie," he says in a deep voice.

My relief is so great it feels as if my knees may give out. Before I know what's happening, he pulls me into a hug.

I try to push away but he holds tighter and whispers in my ear, "Make this look real. We're a couple traveling together."

Understanding, I return his smile when he lets me go. To anyone looking on, we're just a boyfriend and girlfriend happy to be reunited.

He takes my bag. "Any other luggage?"

"No."

Offering me his arm, he leads me to passport control. "Damian will be so happy to see you."

I know he's only making conversation to help me stay calm. Nodding, I look over my shoulder.

"Act normally," he says, squeezing my hand that rests on his arm. "Just relax."

Easier said than done. I'm expecting Maxime's men to burst through the doors with automatic rifles and kill Russell before dragging me away.

"Who am I, anyway?" I asked in hushed tone.

He glances around before handing me the brochure he was reading. I flip it open to find a South African passport with the familiar green cover inside. Turning the page, I read the name next to my photo, Amanda Clifford.

"I'm Devon Edgar," he says in my ear, pretending to sneak in a kiss. "We spent ten days at the Blue Voile on the French Riviera, our first holiday in France."

The information threatens to scatter with how much I'm stressing. Blue Voile. French Riviera. Ten days. Devon Edgar. I repeat it silently in my head.

"You'll be fine," he says with another easy smile.

We go through the scanners. At the customs counter, I remove my sunglasses. The officer looks from my passport to my face with a bored expression. Taking his time, he pages through the passport. The pages look used—frequently touched and full of stamps.

"Returning home?" he asks me in English.

In a reflex reaction, I almost reply in French, but bite my tongue just in time. "Yes." I smile. "Unfortunately, all good things must come to an end."

The officer turns to Russell. "What was the nature of your visit?"

"Holiday," Russell says.

I nearly sag in relief when the officer pounds the stamp in my passport and shifts it toward me over the counter.

"Thank you," I say in a chirpy voice.

"We're not in the clear yet," Russell says as he steers me to the international lounge. "Not until we're in the air."

I'm very aware of that. A powerful man like Maxime will be able to delay flights and search planes. Since I'm unable to sit still, we wander through the duty-free shops where Russell buys wine and truffle oil.

"Really?" I ask as he bags the goods.

He shrugs. "Just trying to look normal."

"Are you a gourmand?"

He grins. "I like to eat."

I can't help but glance at the biceps stretching the arms of his suit jacket. "You don't say."

He places a hand on my arm to silence me as he listens to an announcement. "That's us."

I close my eyes. "Oh, thank God."

"Come." Taking my hand, he leads me to the boarding gate.

My scalp pricks with uneasiness. By now Maxime must know I'm on the run. It feels as if ants are marching down my spine, but ten minutes later, I'm seated in the plane. Russell puts my bag in the overhead storage compartment before sitting down next to me. Gripping the armrests, I stare through the window. I'm nervous about flying. Technically, this is my third flight, but Maxime drugged me during the first one—I don't recall any of it—and during the second I was too preoccupied with my fate to worry about the plane dropping out of the air.

"It's not my business," Russell says, "but I'm going to ask anyway. Are you okay?"

I look at him. Am I? No. I doubt I'll ever be. There are things I can't un-live, feelings I can't undo.

It takes some courage and strength to produce a smile. "Yes. I'm okay now."

"Good." He pats my hand. "Maybe try to get some sleep. You look like you need it."

"I'm not sure I'll be able to sleep." Ever again.

"I'm here to watch over you. I'm not going to let anything happen to you."

"Thanks," I say, meaning it like never before.

It's not until we take off and the wheels fold under the plane that I relax somewhat. It's only then that I let the emotions catch up with me. Loneliness when you're single is unpleasant but hopeful. Loneliness when you love with all your heart and soul is like walking through fire. It burns yet leaves you cold. The cavity of my chest is hollow. Empty. Only the echoes of painful memories are left.

As the view of Marseille slowly shrinks, I say goodbye to Zoe Hart. When we break through the fluffy clouds, I close the door on the life that lies below.

It's only then I allow myself to cry.

~ TO BE CONTINUED ~

ALSO BY CHARMAINE PAULS

DIAMOND MAGNATE NOVELS

(Dark Romance)

Standalone Novel

(Dark Forced Marriage Romance)

Beauty in the Broken

Diamonds are Forever Trilogy

(Dark Mafia Romance)

Diamonds in the Dust

Diamonds in the Rough

Diamonds are Forever

Box Set

Beauty in the Stolen Trilogy

(Dark Romance)

Stolen Lust

Stolen Life

Stolen Love

Box Set

The White Nights Duet

(Contemporary Romance)

White Nights

Midnight Days

The Loan Shark Duet

(Dark Mafia Romance)

Dubious

Consent

Box Set

The Age Between Us Duet

(Older Woman Younger Man Romance)

Old Enough

Young Enough

Box Set

Standalone Novels

(Enemies-to-Lovers Dark Romance)

Darker Than Love

(Second Chance Romance)

Catch Me Twice

Krinar World Novels

(Futuristic Romance)

The Krinar Experiment

The Krinar's Informant

7 Forbidden Arts Series

(Fated Mates Paranormal Romance)

Pyromancist (Fire)

Aeromancist, The Beginning (Prequel)

Aeromancist (Air)

Hydromancist (Water)

Geomancist (Earth)

Necromancist (Spirit)

ABOUT THE AUTHOR

Charmaine Pauls was born in Bloemfontein, South Africa. She obtained a degree in Communication at the University of Potchefstroom and followed a diverse career path in journalism, public relations, advertising, communication, and brand marketing. Her writing has always been an integral part of her professions.

When she moved to Chile with her French husband, she started writing full-time. She has been publishing novels and short stories since 2011. Charmaine currently lives in Montpellier, France with her family. Their household is a lively mix of Afrikaans, English, French, and Spanish.

Join Charmaine's mailing list
https://charmainepauls.com/subscribe/

Join Charmaine's readers' group on Facebook
http://bit.ly/CPaulsFBGroup

Read more about Charmaine's novels and short stories on
https://charmainepauls.com

Connect with Charmaine

Facebook
http://bit.ly/Charmaine-Pauls-Facebook

Amazon
http://bit.ly/Charmaine-Pauls-Amazon

Goodreads
http://bit.ly/Charmaine-Pauls-Goodreads

Twitter
https://twitter.com/CharmainePauls

Instagram
https://instagram.com/charmainepaulsbooks

BookBub
http://bit.ly/CPaulsBB

TikTok
https://www.tiktok.com/@charmainepauls

Made in the USA
Columbia, SC
08 March 2022